DESIGNATED ASSASSIN

Isolated in the mountains of Mourne, far from the lonely Ulster crossroads where it all began, a deadly final reckoning is in the making. Charles Garrett, lethal executive arm of the British government organisation PACT, wants revenge on the IRA assassin who mowed down his wife in a hail of bullets. Lured into a trap by a series of brutal assassinations of MI5 couriers — Garrett discovers that the ultimate enemy is within. And that only he who dares . . .

FREDERICK NOLAN

DESIGNATED ASSASSIN

Complete and Unabridged

LINFORD
Leicester

First published in Great Britain

First Linford Edition
published 2008

British Library CIP Data

Nolan, Frederick, *1931* –
   Designated assassin.—Large print ed.—
Linford mystery library
   1. Secret service—Fiction 2. Suspense fiction
3. Large type books
I. Title
823.9'14 [F]

ISBN 978–1–84782–410–3

Published by
F. A. Thorpe (Publishing)
Anstey, Leicestershire

Set by Words & Graphics Ltd.
Anstey, Leicestershire
Printed and bound in Great Britain by
T. J. International Ltd., Padstow, Cornwall

This book is printed on acid-free paper

For Jan, Lisa and especially Rory

1

Jessica Goldman slid out of the terry beach coat and lay back on the bed. Her body was already beautifully tanned from the spring sun. They kissed, and Garrett felt the familiar sensation of slow surrender. She eeled out of his arms and went across to the window, closing the venetian blinds. He heard the soft slither of the swimsuit as she took it off and then she was in his arms again, naked. He could smell the familiar warm perfume of her skin. Her lips were slightly parted, her eyes closed. She sighed when he touched her. She put her hands inside his shirt, pulling his body hard against hers.

'Be genital with me,' she said, and they burst out laughing.

They had decided on an early holiday: May, Jessica said, so that they could beat the tourists. They flew to Athens and then took the Olympic thirty-seater that made the hop across the ninety nautical miles east to Mykonos. Twenty-three square miles in area, most of it as barren as a donkey's foot, Mykonos is to the Greek islands what St Tropez is to the south of France. In the summer it bulges at every seam with tourists: jet-setters and backpackers, honeymooners and moonlighters and — everywhere — gay couples. This early in the year, however, its colourful maze of streets was still uncrowded, and Garrett experienced no trouble in booking a comfortable double on the top floor of the Hotel Lito.

Each room had its own balcony looking out across the bay and the town of Hora, a white jumble of buildings and dome-topped churches that stretched in a semicircle below. A small fleet of fishing boats bobbed at anchor in the sheltered harbour; each evening, cruise boats docked in a blaze of lights and sirens. The wife of the owner of the hotel was a plump, dark-haired lady who sang melodiously as she served breakfast: slices of cheese and pressed ham, yoghurt with honey, rolls and coffee.

'What do you suppose the rest of the

world is doing right now?' Jessica said.

'Reading about us in *People* magazine,' Garrett replied. 'Consumed with envy.'

Every evening they sat on the balcony with a glass of Cava Boutari and watched the sun go down. Then they would stroll into town, taking their time about it. They ate at Alexander's on the seafront, at a seafood place called Spyros, tucked in a rocky corner beneath the three windmills which dominated the hill to the south of town, or at one of the open-air tavernas around the market square. By the end of their first week, they had explored most of the town's narrow maze of streets.

'How do you feel about a sea trip?' Jessica asked.

'What did you have in mind?'

'There's a ferry service between the islands,' Jessica told him. 'We could go to Andros or Tinos, stay over a night, come back the next day. It seems a shame to come to the Greek islands and only see one.'

'We could rent a sailing boat, if you like. Just the two of us.'

'I know. But just this once, let's be grockles.'

They booked tickets in the travel agency near the cathedral, and early next morning went down to the quay to mingle with the milling crowd of tourists waiting to join the ferry. The boat looked familiar, and it was a while before Garrett realized she looked very much like one of the old pleasure boats that still ply the Danube at Budapest, a big, white-painted, single-funnel steamer with a glassed-in promenade deck and rows of seats beneath a canvas canopy in the stern.

The boat left the harbour in a flurry of water and fussy hoots; the fishing boats anchored in the bay bobbed like ducks on the waves she made, her blunt nose pointing west. After a while Mykonos dropped below the horizon and there was nothing to look at but the swelling movement of the wine dark sea.

The journey to Paros would take about another two hours, Jessica had said. Garrett got up and wandered forward, where the smell of coffee from the little

4

snack bar on the promenade deck had attracted a cluster of buyers. The boat was bucking a little on the waves now, and one or two of the people who had embarked at Mykonos were no longer smiling quite so happily. He frowned as his reverie was interrupted. The steady drum of the engines had altered, easing to a lighter, less urgent sound. The speed fell away and the boat wallowed a little in the swell.

'Attention, everyone! Attention!'

The metallic voice blasted from a speaker above Garrett's head.

Garrett moved rapidly from amidships towards the stern of the boat, where Jessica was still reading her short stories. Like many of the other passengers, she was not really paying any attention to the strident voice on the public-address system.

'Attention, attention! All passengers attention! This ship is now under the command of the Palestinian West Bank Liberation Faction! This ship is now in our hands! Everyone will remain exactly where they are! Everyone remain still!

Anyone who disobeys will be shot!'

'What's going on?' an elderly woman said, irritation in her voice. 'What's all this noise about?'

As if to answer her question, two men came along the deck toward the stern. Both of them were dark-haired, swarthy, casually dressed, one in a white shirt, light cotton trousers and trainers, the other in a dark blue sports shirt, jeans and cheap canvas shoes. Both carried what looked like 9 mm Uzi sub-machine-guns with 32-round magazines. One of them jumped on to a bench.

'Ev'body siddown!' he shouted. 'Ev'body siddown onna floor!'

'Excuse me, please,' one of the German tourists said. 'Can we — '

'Siddownonna floor!' the man with the gun screamed. 'Now!'

He pointed the Uzi at the sky and fired a burst. The bullets tore the canvas canopy above his head to shreds. Someone screamed. The passengers cowered on the floor, some of them with their hands over their heads, others looking up in terror at the empty, hating faces of the men with the guns. Garrett sat with his back against the ship's rail near the flagpole at the stern, Jessica beside him. He could feel her trembling, and knew why; it was not so long since she had nearly died at the hands of another terrorist. She turned her head so that her lips were close to his ear.

'What do they want?'

'I don't know,' he said, but he knew. There could only be one reason for this piracy. Whoever these people were, they needed hostages to bargain for whatever it was they wanted. He risked squinting up. The two terrorists were watching their prisoners with casual contempt. They were sloppy; that was good, he thought.

'Attention all passengers, attention!'

The boat was entirely silent now, and it was easy to hear the harsh voice on the PA system.

'You are all prisoners of war! You will all do exactly as you are told! Anyone who disobeys will be instantly shot! Make no mistake! Do exactly as you are told, or you will be shot!'

'Oh, my Gahd,' an American voice

whimpered. 'Oh, my Gahd, Harry!'

'Quiet!' one of the terrorists shouted. 'Quiet!'

Minutes ticked away, then half an hour. The boat was hove to, with just enough way on her to keep her from broaching. Garrett tried to remember the exact layout of the vessel. There were three decks: one below them was the salon, which ran almost the whole length of the ship. Fore and aft stairways led up from it to the glassed-in promenade deck, with the bridge at its forward end. It continued aft to the canopied area where he and Jessica were now prisoners. Forward, beneath the glassed-in area, two more stairways ascended to the boat deck, which was open to the elements. How many terrorists? he thought. These two, two more below, one or two holding the captain and crew at gunpoint? Five or six of them at least. Not good news.

The PA system crackled, and he heard the fuff-fuff sound of someone testing a microphone.

'Ladies and gentlemen, this is Captain Karamanlis speaking.' The voice was edgy, thin with uncertainty. 'I have to tell you that the ship is in the hands of the West Bank Liberation Faction. I ask you all to do exactly as you are told. These . . . these people have made certain . . . demands. The government. The Greek government . . . we are awaiting a reply. Please have patience. There is no danger as long as you co-operate.'

The amplifier crackled and went silent.

Garrett felt Jessica's hand on his arm, holding him very tightly. He put his hands on hers; she was as cold as ice, and he knew she was reliving those terrible hours she had spent as a prisoner of the Arab terrorist Leila Jarhoun.

Will I forget, Charles? Will I ever forget?

Yes, he had lied. *You'll forget.*

You never forgot. He knew that only too well.

'Attention, attention! This is Achmet. I am the commander of this unit. In the name of God, the compassionate, the merciful. The best honour is dying in the name of Allah. Stubbornness and close-mindedness of Israel authorities will exceed us to more determination and stressing our conditions which sum up the immediate release of our brothers held in Israel. At the same time will be the immediate release of all the passengers of this ship.'

'What did he say?' the elderly woman who had spoken before asked, her voice querulous. 'I can't understand what he's saying.'

'Shhhh!' someone told her. The terrorist leader was still speaking.

' . . . we will not accept postponing to take place. We don't fear death, the whole world knows we are not afraid. For your information, this boat has been planted with explosive activated by high technical devices. If our demands are not met by 12:30 hours we are going to kill one passenger. Then another every half-hour after. Now we honestly request the Israeli government to act as an independent country and to liberate itself from the yoke of the United States.'

'Did he say he was going to kill someone?' the elderly woman said, disbelievingly. 'Did that man say — '

'If I was you, I'd shut up, lady,' one of the young backpackers told her, his voice tense. 'Don't draw attention to yourself.'

Jessica touched Garrett's arm. When he turned, she gestured with her head and he looked out across the sea on the starboard side of the ship. A sleek grey Greek naval destroyer had slid into sight, well out of range of any gun the terrorists might possess. Almost at the same time, they heard the whistling chatter of a helicopter making a pass over the ship. Some of the passengers raised a ragged cheer, but Garrett knew it was premature. There would be no rescue attempt while Achmet and his men held the several hundred passengers on board the *Aphrodite* hostage. The destroyer and helicopter were simply keeping the ship under surveillance while the real negotiating was conducted on ship-to-shore radio.

Garrett looked at his watch: 12:25. The PA system hissed emptily. A strange air of tension mixed with resignation seemed to have settled over the huddled group of passengers beneath the tattered canopy in the stern of the ship. People acted

11

strangely in such situations. He watched the two terrorists standing on the seats. One of them said something to the other in Arabic. The second man laughed. When he replied he accompanied his words with the throat-slitting gesture.

'What did he say?' Jessica whispered in Garrett's ear. He shook his head.

'I didn't hear,' he lied. The first man had said that Achmet was wasting his time talking. The second man laughed. 'Only one way to convince them,' he had said, and drew a forefinger across his throat.

Garrett looked at his watch again. 12:32. Screams broke into the silence. There was a commotion below. Two men came up the stairway dragging a swarthy, portly, dark-haired man of about forty. As they hauled him up on to the open sun deck, he began screaming.

'Help me, help me! For God's sake, help me. They're going to kill me! Help me, help me!'

Nobody moved. The terrorists took the man over to the rail on the starboard side of the boat, where their every movement would be visible to the watchers on the Greek destroyer a quarter of a mile away. Every eye was fixed on the three men. Garrett very carefully gathered his legs under him in a crouching squat as the two terrorists guarding the passengers under the canopy turned to watch. In the same second that the two men on the boat deck executed the first passenger and let his body fall forward and down to the sea, Garrett moved.

He sprang forward and up, his left arm going round the nearest man's neck, yanking his head back while his right hand slid the blade of the knife under the man's ribcage and up into his heart. Even as the terrorist's knees buckled, Garrett had the Uzi out of the dying man's hands, cocked and ready to fire. The other terrorist whirled in astonished alarm, eyes wide with panic as he loosed off an arcing burst from the machine gun. As the bullets from the Uzi tore into the body of the dead terrorist shielding him, Garrett fired six bullets into the man facing him, knocking him backwards and sideways. He was dead even as he fell, the gun clattering to the deck.

The passengers scrabbled away from danger as Garrett scooped up the Uzi and ran beneath the canopy to the foot of the companionway leading to the upper deck, firing both weapons upwards at the two killers. Both men died instantly. Garrett did not spare their slumped bodies a second glance. He went down the stairs into the main salon two at a time, yelling at everyone to get down on the floor and stay there.

Screaming women dragged their children to the deck, men shouted and scuffled. Others stared at Garrett as if the big man was an apparition. Someone stood in the aisle, holding up his hand like a traffic policeman, shouting something in Greek. Garrett short-armed him aside and hurried forward to the companionway leading up to the bridge, taking the steps two at a time, and skidded to a stop outside a door with a sign in Greek that said 'No entry for unauthorized personnel'.

He took twenty seconds to get his

breathing under control, trying to remember everything he had learned during his training as one of the élite members of the 14th Intelligence Unit in the 'killing room' at the Hereford headquarters of the Special Air Service. *Hostages will be under restraint, seated or on the floor. Anyone standing is a target. Your hostile movement will trigger theirs; kill anything that moves.*

He did not bother to try the handle of the door leading on to the bridge; it would be locked on the inside. Like all ship doors, it would open outwards; that, too, was a small factor in his favour. He banged hard on the door with his fist.

'Achmet, Achmet, open up!' he shouted in Arabic. 'Open up!'

He heard voices inside; the lock turned and the door opened cautiously. As it inched open, Garrett took hold of the ring-pull handle and yanked it back with all his strength. A young man of about twenty-five, dark-haired, fell out across the high coaming across the doorway. Without hesitation, Garrett shot him in the back of the head and went in through

15

the door, not even breaking his stride.

Seconds were like eons: he saw the startled faces of the ship's officers, their bodies frozen with fear and indecision, and the bearded figure by the radio desk grabbing the gun stuck in his belt, eyes narrowed with tension and surprise. *Achmet*, Garrett thought, instinctively pressing the trigger. Achmet's angry expression turned to blank shock as the murderous burst of fire from the Uzi smashed the life out of his body, hurling him back against the wall, the front of his chest in bloody tatters. He opened his mouth as if to say something, then slid down to the floor, leaving a ghastly red smear on the cream-painted metal wall. The 9 mm Beretta he had tried to use slid from his nerveless hands. Garrett kicked it away to the other side of the room. The reek of cordite mingled with the bright copper stink of death.

'How many of them are there?' Garrett shouted, his voice harsher than he could have imagined. The officer nearest to him flinched as if he had been struck physically.

'Six, there were six,' the smallest of the three men on the bridge told him.

'You're sure?'

'That was what he . . . ' The man gestured at the fallen terrorist leader. 'That was what he said.'

'You're Captain Karamanlis?'

'Y-y-y-yes,' the small man said. He was in his mid-fifties, a portly, greying, handsome man in a well-cut uniform with lots of gold braid on it. 'Ka-ka-kara-kara-manlis.' He was shaking. Garrett put his hand on the captain's shoulder.

'You'd better pull yourself together, Captain,' he said. 'Get on the PA. Tell your passengers the danger is over.'

Karamanlis looked at him for a long moment, as if uncomprehending. Then he blinked rapidly several times.

'You killed them all?' he whispered. 'All of them?'

'They needed killing,' Garrett replied.

2

Maurice Abernethy was not a vain man, but he prided himself upon the concision of his speech, on the brevity of his reports and upon his reliability as a courier. He had been a security service courier for nearly as long as Her Majesty Queen Elizabeth II had been on the throne of England and he considered he did and had done his duty with the same professional devotion that she did and had done hers. He was a tall, thin man with a rather long jaw and lacklustre brown hair that he parted on the left-hand side. He invariably dressed in a suit, usually a dark blue or a charcoal-grey pinstripe, with a lightly starched white shirt and the striped tie of either his club, White's, or his old school, Wellington.

When he was not travelling abroad, Maurice Abernethy caught the fast 8:34 London train every morning, doing most of *The Times* crossword in the twenty-five minutes it took to reach Baker Street; there was usually a short wait for the Jubilee Line train to Bond Street, so he often had it finished by the time he got there. He always walked to Curzon Street by the same route: straight down Davies Street and around the west side of Berkeley Square to the senior staff entrance on Fitzmaurice Place. He arrived almost on the stroke of 9:30. The Curzon Street House commissionaires often said you could set your clock by Mr Abernethy.

At ten o'clock every morning all couriers not actually in transit assembled in the routing officer's office to receive their assignments.

The RO was a genial Welshman named Hugh Thomas, known to all and sundry as 'Dylan'.

His voice went up and down like the hills and valleys of his native Gwent.

'Good morning, *rhyfelwyr*,' he said, taking his seat at the desk facing them. 'All well, I trust?'

His 'soldiers', as he called them in

Welsh, chorused their agreement. He beamed at them and spread the assignment dockets on the desk in front of him. Peter Cavenham, one of the more senior messengers, leaned forward in his chair.

'All right, Dylan,' he said conspiratorially. 'Just give me Mauritius and I'll be on my way.'

'No Mauritius for you, boyo,' Dylan grinned. 'Melbourne, isn't it?'

Cavenham groaned. 'Melbourne,' he said, with exaggerated dismay. 'The Manchester of Australia.'

'Could be worse, Peter,' Harry Peterson said. 'You could have got Santiago.'

'Or Bogotá,' someone else chimed in. 'There's a fun place.'

Abernethy waited patiently as Dylan handed out the assignments. Each man was given a folder which contained all the necessary travel documents, foreign currency where necessary (although each courier carried an Amex Gold Card) and a wax-sealed envelope which contained a DR — designated recipient — docket that had to be signed by that recipient and returned in an identically sealed envelope.

Paperclipped to each folder was a small square of card with a coded number on it. On receiving his allocation, each courier took this to the duty desk so numbered, and there collected the standard DI5 leather briefcase that he was to deliver. This would be given to him with its combination locks already closed, and handcuffed to his wrist by the duty officer at that desk. It would remain that way until the messenger reached his destination; only the DR there had a key.

'Pemberton, Athens,' Dylan called out. 'Stevens, Tel Aviv.'

Abernethy lit a cigarette and waited. He'd been hoping for a decent assignment but most of the good ones had already gone. It would be just his luck to get something really dull, like Stockholm or Helsinki.

'Abernethy, Belfast,' Dylan said, looking up. Abernethy shrugged and went over for his folder. The number on the red square of card was D6A-12. D Branch was and always had been counterespionage, Soviets, and D6A was Northern Ireland. That meant he would probably be couriering secret documents for one of the four 'desks' dealing with KGB activities there. Abernethy permitted himself a small smile. You couldn't work in Five for as long as he had without learning something about the way the business worked. At ten-thirty, he put on his Burberry, picked up his hat and went up to the fourth floor, where he reported to the duty officer on A-12, a neatly groomed, compactly built man of about thirty-five.

'Ah, Mr Abernethy,' the man said, his manner brisk. 'I'm Mick Jarvis. You all set for Belfast?'

'I'm on BA 4592, Super Shuttle from Heathrow,' Abernethy recited. 'Leaves twelve-thirty, arrives Belfast thirteen-forty hours.'

He held out his right hand, cuff pulled back, and Jarvis slid the cold metal jaw round his wrist, sliding it snugly shut.

'Comfortable?'

'Fine,' Abernethy said, picking up the bulky briefcase.

'Don't lose that,' Jarvis grinned. Abernethy did not deign to reply; such facetiousness deserved to be ignored. He went along the corridor to the central foyer and took the lift down to the lower ground floor level. One of the DI5 taxi fleet saw him coming out of the doors and pulled up in front of the entrance.

'It's Mr Abernethy, isn't it?' the driver said. 'Morning, guv.'

'Hullo, George,' Abernethy said.

'Goin' anywhere nice?'

Abernethy shook his head. 'Terminal One, Heathrow, please.'

George shrugged and drove up the ramp and out into Curzon Street, becoming at once just another London taxicab taking just another London businessman to the airport. Although the traffic was quite heavy, George was an old hand at weaving his way through it, and the journey took little more than thirty-five minutes. Abernethy went into the terminal, ignoring the check-in desks, and took the stairs to the balcony level. He walked without haste along the corridor until he came to an unmarked door, which he opened with a plastic strip not unlike a credit card. He stepped into the diplomatic lounge, which was empty except for a smiling stewardess. While she took care of the paperwork, he poured himself a cup of coffee from the Cona simmering on a sideboard and sat down by the window to read *The Economist* until they told him the plane was ready to board.

The Boeing 757 was a spacious and comfortable plane, and as they flew northwest the weather grew fine and clear. Liverpool spread like a map off to the right, the Mersey bright in the afternoon sunshine, the coastline bending around from Southport all the way up to Blackpool. After a while they passed over the southern end of the Isle of Man, and a little later the pilot put the plane into the wide left-hand bank that would take it out over the harbour, the city of Belfast on his left as he made his final approach to Aldergrove.

Abernethy remained in his seat, reading, as the other passengers shuffled their way out of the plane. When everyone else was off, he got up and followed the stewardess down a stairway just inside the terminal to the tarmac, where an unmarked security service car was waiting with its engine running. He showed the driver his ID, and got in. The driver moved slowly towards the special clearance exit, which was manned by armed soldiers. They waved the car through into the enclosed security channel through which all cars, even this one, were required to pass.

'Lisburn, is it, sir?' the driver asked, as he negotiated the anti-speed ramps. Abernethy nodded absently.

'Been a big pile-up on the motorway, you see,' the driver told him. 'Don't know how long it'll take them to clear it.'

'Are both carriageways blocked?'

'Yes, sir. It was a tanker. Fuel oil all over the road.'

Abernethy leaned forward. 'Is there another route?'

'We might do better to go through Dunrod,' the driver said.

'Very well,' Abernethy told him. 'Give it a try.'

It was only about thirteen miles from Aldergrove to the centre of Lisburn, the two-lane B39 as straight as a ruled line until Clady Corner, where it joined the main A52 highway to Belfast. There the driver would have to cut back to Boomer's Bridge and get on to the narrow B101, skirting the western flank of Bo Hill, running southward between Boomer's Hill and White Mountain with their old quarries and then dropping down into the huddled northern suburbs of Lisburn.

Hardly an inspiring journey, Abernethy thought, but then, there were very few places in the world where the drive in from the airport was. He tried to think of one: Naples, perhaps, in the days before the *autostrada*, when you came over the via Nova del Campo di Marte with that fantastic view, Capri blue and clear on the horizon, and the sun suddenly striking hot through the windscreen of the car. Or —

'I'll need to stop for a moment, sir,' the driver said. 'Call of nature.'

Abernethy frowned. 'Very well,' he said. He looked out of the window. They were on the B101 somewhere between

Cochranstown and Rock House; yes, there was the Leathemstown Reservoir on the right. Just up ahead on their left, beneath the marching strands of electricity cables looping from north to south, was a lay-by. The driver pulled in and stopped, got out of the car, and disappeared behind the trees fringing the river that flowed into the reservation beneath the culvert under the road.

Abernethy noticed a nondescript Ford Transit parked about thirty yards away. As he watched, a man in blue overalls got out of the truck, opened the rear doors and took out what looked like a length of drainpipe. It was only when he set it on his shoulder that Maurice Abernethy realized what it actually was, and by that time it was far too late for him to do anything but watch, paralysed by terror, as the man launched the rocket straight at him.

The weapon was a Soviet-made RPG-2 portable rocket launcher, itself developed from the German Panzerfaust of World War Two. It fired a fin-stabilized HEAT projectile with an 82-mm warhead weighing nearly two kilos and capable of penetrating up to 180 mm of armour. The rocket explosion killed Maurice Abernethy instantly, turning the car into a blazing fireball of twisted junk. Huge black coils of smoke rose into the pale blue springtime sky. As the man who had fired the rocket unhurriedly put the launcher back into the truck, the driver came trotting up the hill from the river and got into the passenger seat of the Transit. The two men drove away without so much as a backward look.

★ ★ ★

Two hours later, the news editor of the *Belfast Telegraph* took a call in his office on Royal Avenue. The speaker was a man with a local accent who told the editor that the death of Maurice Abernethy had been an act of political assassination.

'Are you claiming responsibility for this . . . assassination?' the editor asked.

'Aye, we are,' the man said. 'See that they hear about it in the Rathole.' Northern Ireland Headquarters, the fortified complex of buildings in Lisburn occupied by the security services, was known only to insiders as the Rathole; this was clearly no hoax call.

'Who are you?' the editor asked.

'Just tell them Sean Hennessy called it in,' the man said. 'And that they'll be hearing from me again.'

3

The interrogation room was roughly twelve feet by eight, two of its walls painted cream, the others insulated with a material that resembled polystyrene. The window was blacked out, reinforced with wire and protected by bars. A table and four moulded chairs stood in the centre of the room, which was brightly lit by a fluorescent panel let into the ceiling. The concrete floor was stained or painted red. There was no light switch and no handle on the inside of the door.

Charlie Tarr was brought down from his cell by a detective dressed in a dark suit with a grubby dark blue shirt and striped tie. He hustled Tarr into the room and pushed him over towards the table, where another man was already sitting.

'This him, is it?' the man said, leaning back with his arms dangling down behind the chair.

He was running to fat, with greasy

dark brown hair that lay flat on his head. His face was expressionless, his eyes empty with boredom. He wore a cheap imitation-leather bomber jacket and jeans held up with a wide leather belt with a heavy brass buckle that his beer gut bulged over.

'What's this all about?' Tarr asked. 'Who are you?'

'We ask the questions, sonny,' the one in the suit said, sliding into a chair next to Tarr. 'You just answer. Got it?'

'He's got it, all right,' the fat one said. 'He knows why he's here, don't you?'

'I haven't got a clue,' Tarr said.

The fat one smiled without humour. 'We'll give you one, then,' he said. 'See this form on the table?'

'I see it. I can't read.'

'You're illiterate?' The two men exchanged glances.

'Aye,' Charlie said. He was longing for a cigarette but he knew better than to ask for one.

'Who are you running around with these days, Charlie?'

'You mean drinking mates?'

'For instance.'

'Jimmy Adams. Leslie Barton. Charlie Lomax.'

'You don't think we're buying that, do you?' the fat one said angrily.

'No use trying to foist us off with people you know won't get you into trouble, sonny,' the other one said. 'The rest of your pals are already in here. Six of them, Charlie. There's only one missing now. You know who we mean.'

'I don't know who you mean. How can I know who you mean if I don't know who you've got in here?'

'We'll tell you, laddie,' the one in the suit said. 'We'll tell you. We've got Billy Johnson. Gerry Hampson. Jack Dempsey. Ronnie Grice. Robbie Robinson. Georgie Lee. Now we've got them, you might as well tell us the rest of it.'

'I still don't know what you mean.'

'It was Monday,' Leather Jacket continued. 'And you went up to Leathemstown Reservoir and waited for someone to come along in a car. And then you blew him up. With a fucking bazooka.'

'Not me, sor. Definitely not.'

'All you have to do is tell us what happened. Who set it up. We'll write it down and then you can sign it. I promise you we'll do our best for you.'

Tarr shook his head and stared at the floor.

'Where do you drink?' Suit asked abruptly.

'Lots of places.'

'What about Ferndale Road Social Club? You a member?'

'Yes, I am.'

'You know that's where the truck for the job we're talking about was stolen?'

'No, sor.'

'You're a fuckin' liar. You met someone in the Ferndale Road club. You were given the rocket launcher and told what to do. They told you he was a security agent, didn't they? Of course, he wasn't.'

'I'm not guilty. Not guilty.'

'You're not in court,' Suit snapped. 'In here, you say you have nothing to say. Understand?'

'Yes, sor.'

'I'll put it to you again,' Leather Jacket said. 'After you got the rocket launcher you got into the truck. A stolen Ford Transit, registration N586 BYO. You drove up to the reservoir and did the job.'

'No, sor, I never.'

'I'm going to give you some time to think it over,' Leather Jacket said. 'Think very hard and let us know. It's up to you. You're going down, either way. It's only whether you do twenty years or six. You let us know, right?'

'Yes, sor,' Tarr said. The interview had lasted two hours. He was glad to get out of the stifling room. When he got back to his cell they brought him some tea. He didn't drink it in case they'd put something in it. You never knew. Half an hour later the door opened again and another detective came in. He jerked his thumb at the door and Tarr got up.

'What now?' he said.

The detective did not answer but grabbed his upper arm and hustled him along the corridor and down the stairs back to the interview room. Another man sat where Leather Jacket had been sitting. This one was strongly built, with a thick-lipped, ruddy face and gingery hair.

'Right,' he said. 'Sit down and let's get started.' His voice was harsh and hostile. The detective who had brought Tarr down from his cell sat on his right.

'No more jacking off,' the ginger-haired one said. 'We want the information. What about this murder?'

'Nothing to say. Not guilty, sor.'

'Look, son,' the ginger-haired detective said, his manner that of a man who is doing his best to keep his temper in check. 'You are not a hard man. You won't last the time in here. We'll break you like a fuckin' twig if you make us. So do it the easy way. Take my advice, cough.'

Tarr shook his head. 'I got nothing to say.'

The detective sitting beside him stood up and went behind him.

'You've got plenty to say,' he said, and as he said it, he hit the seated man across the back of the head. He repeated the words and the blow six or eight times, dispassionate as a surgeon.

'Don't get him cross, son,' the ginger-haired one told him. 'He's a bugger when he's roused. You better tell us what we want to know.'

‘I can't tell you what I don't know. I wasn't there. I never done it.'

‘But you're guilty, son,' the detective standing behind Tarr said. ‘You're guilty and you're going down for it. Stand up!'

Tarr stood up. The man standing behind him hit him in the kidneys. He fell forward across the table. The ginger-haired man slammed the flat of his hand down hard on the side of Tarr's head, smashing it against the table, then jerked him upright by the hair. The two detectives pushed him against the polystyrene-insulated wall, and one of them hit him hard in the belly. He doubled over, retching. The second one straightened him up, and the first man hit him again. They kept on doing that for some time until he collapsed on the floor. Then they picked him up and sat him down. Great spasms of pain and fear racking his body, Tarr lolled sideways and nearly fell off the chair. The ginger-haired detective slapped his face lightly.

‘Don't pass out,' he said, a warning in

his voice. 'You hear me? Don't fuckin' dare pass out.'

'Nothing to say,' Tarr groaned. 'Nothing to say.'

The ginger-haired detective lifted him to his feet and threw him face first against the wall. He cannoned off it and fell to the floor. They picked him up and did it again, and again, and again. When they let go of him he collapsed on the floor, moaning with pain, knees drawn up to his belly. Hands grabbed him again and he screamed, but this time they only sat him on the chair. Through swollen eyes Tarr saw that another man had come into the room. He was tall and thin, with bushy brown hair and a long jaw. His eyes were covered by blue-tinted sunglasses. He wore a green camouflage Army battle-dress and carried a riding crop which he flicked against the side of his leg from time to time.

'All right,' he said. 'Outside.'

The two detectives went out of the interrogation room and the officer came and sat down on the chair opposite Tarr. He shook his head sadly.

'You're lucky I came in,' he said. 'Those two would have killed you.'

He handed Tarr a polystyrene cup half full of tepid tea. Tarr gulped it down, then wiped his mouth with the back of a trembling hand.

'You'd better wise up, laddybuck,' the officer said. 'You're detained under the Prevention of Terrorism Act. We can keep you in here for seven days. Just think about that. Think about going through this five times a day. You'd never stand it. Nobody ever does. Why don't you just tell me all about it? I'll write down what you say and you can sign it.'

'But I haven't done anything,' Tarr keened. 'I haven't done anything.'

'You're wasting my time,' the officer said sharply. He banged on the door of the interview room and the two detectives came back in.

'Up against the wall!' one of them shouted. Tarr got to his feet, shaking. The ginger-haired one grabbed him before he fell.

'Put him down for the night,' the officer said.

'Sir, we — '

'Do what I say. Did you hear me, Tarr? I'm going to put you down for the night. I'm not usually this generous. You have a good think. In the morning we'll discuss it again. You think about what you want to tell me. It's not you I'm after, you know that. It's Hennessy I want. You help me to get him and you won't be sorry.'

They took Charlie Tarr up the iron staircase and shoved him into the detention cell. It had a single bed and a chair. There was no window, just a small aperture maybe eighteen inches square covered with wire mesh high on the wall. The light was a perspex dome with a steel fitment. There was no switch to turn it off. He lay on the bed and tried to sleep. The cell was very hot and his body throbbed with pain. The heat built up until he could bear it no longer. He banged on the door and asked to go to the toilet. It was cool outside, but they did not give him any longer than necessary. He dozed fitfully but did not really sleep. At six-thirty next morning they came for him again.

'Hennessy, Hennessy!' Patterson snapped impatiently. 'What did he say about Hennessy?'

Dressed in the standard green camouflage battledress of a major in the British Army, Harry Patterson set his thin-lipped mouth in an expression of impatience. The anger in his pale blue eyes was almost invisible behind the bluetinted sunglasses he invariably wore.

'Nothing, sir,' his second-in-command, Lieutenant Peter Christie, replied nervously.

'What about the others?'

'We've run them through PDVC here, and R2 in London has had a go, sir,' Christie replied. 'Nothing known. If they're associated with Hennessy, there's no record of it.'

The computer at Northern Ireland Headquarters in Lisburn had four sections. 'P', which stood for 'Personal', contained information on more than eighty per cent of the population of Ulster — name, parentage, address, education, description, occupation, habits, relatives, vehicles used, recorded movements and all known associates.

'D' section — it stood for 'Directory' — was programmed to provide name, occupation, religion, political preference and computer reference code of the occupants of every house in the province, together with a distinguishing mark for that house, such as the colour of the door, the blinds, or the wallpaper in a specified room. Sometimes even the names of dogs were recorded.

'V' section — vehicles — had the registration numbers, makes and colours of motor cars, religion of owners, and recommendations regarding the degree of suspicion appropriate at roadblocks. The fourth section, 'C', provided check-point information, which recorded every time a vehicle was encountered by the security forces in a road check or on any other occasion whatsoever, as well as the names of all parties in the car at the time of the check. The whole system was known as PDVC. It had been absolutely no help at all in identifying the assassins of Maurice Abernethy.

'Then we'll have to break a few more heads, Peter,' Patterson said, banging a fist down on his desk to emphasize his point.

Christie shrugged. There was no percentage in arguing. Patterson was a wild man. Although he had only been in the Province six months, he had already made a deep impression on the terrorists — the filth, as he called them, the unwashed — out there in the mean streets. It was they who had given him his nickname: Qhaddafi.

The RUC interrogators at the Special Interrogation Unit in Castlereagh weren't exactly Shirley Temples, but they weren't in the same bare-knuckle class as Major Harry Patterson's Military Intelligence Unit, known throughout Ulster as 'the Grave-diggers' for reasons that needed no explanation.

'It's bad enough keeping track of what the known filth is doing, without some maverick like Hennessy starting up privately,' Patterson said disgustedly. 'Now London is sending us some fucking hotshot to tell us how the KGB is infiltrating the Provos. When does he arrive, anyway?'

'His name is Bradley. He arrives at Aldergrove at eleven-forty tomorrow morning.'

'You've arranged an escort?'

'Yes, sir. And don't forget the DCI wants to see you in an hour.'

'What d'you suppose he wants?'

'Your guts for garters, I suspect,' a voice drawled from the doorway. The speaker was a tall, balding, well-built man, with a high complexion, almost invisible pale blond eyebrows and pale blue eyes. His full-lipped mouth was twisted in an habitually disdainful sneer.

'Oh hello, Elkins,' Patterson said without enthusiasm. 'What do you want?'

Stephen Elkins, known to everyone in the fortified enclave that housed NIHQ as 'Smooth Steve', was DI5 liaison officer at Lisburn, and as such, responsible for the co-ordination of all counterespionage and undercover operations in the province. He was, in his own special way, as universally detested as Patterson.

'Just came in to see whether your boys actually got anything at all out of the interrogations,' Elkins drawled. 'I haven't seen a report as yet. Has there been one?'

He knew damned well there had not, of course. Reminding Patterson that the required chapter and verse on the 'unfortunate accident' that had resulted in the death of Charlie Tarr had not yet been filed was his unsubtle way of needling him. Elkins made no secret of his disapproval of Patterson's methods. Patterson in turn described Elkins as a 'plonker', a typical product of the British upper classes, all flattened vowels and friends in high places, and about as much use as a punctured condom.

'You'll see it when it's done,' Patterson growled. 'Which will be when I am good and bloody well ready.'

'I hope it's before our friend from the ministry arrives, dear boy,' Elkins said good-naturedly. 'Otherwise I imagine he may, ah, how do you so elegantly put it, kick some arse.'

'Did you actually come in here for any useful purpose, Elkins, or are you just practising flapping your limp wrist?'

'Look, I'll put it into words of one syllable for you,' Elkins said. 'Maurice Abernethy was a DI5 courier. Until we know for sure that the papers he was carrying burned in the car with him, we have to assume they may have fallen into the wrong hands. Which makes any investigation into his death very much the concern of my department. This isn't the right sort of case for your bloody great hobnailed-boot technique, and I won't have it being used without my sanction.'

'Your sanction doesn't amount to what a fly leaves on a wall in here, Elkins,' Patterson told him. 'You'd better leave this to the big boys.'

'We did,' Elkins said, colouring angrily. 'And look where that got us.'

'You seem to be having trouble with the English language today, *old boy*,' Patterson said. 'So I'll spell it out for you. You can't frighten these hard men by flapping perfumed hankies at them. The only thing they understand is strength. Leave this to us. The Army will find out who killed Maurice Abernethy. And the Army will take care of them.'

Elkins drew in his breath and then let it out in an exasperated rush.

'I can see I'm wasting my time being polite,' he snapped. 'So I'll make this formal. It is now two o'clock. I'll give you two hours to have that report on my desk. If it isn't there by then, I shall be drafting a report of my own for the Director General in London, recommending your removal.'

'Fire away,' Patterson said contemptuously. 'I don't take my orders from Curzon Street.'

Elkins stared at him for a long moment, then shook his head in disgust. 'I don't know what you do to the enemy, Patterson,' he said. 'But by God, you frighten me.'

He swung about and went out of the office, slamming the door so hard that a book fell off the shelf next to it. Christie went across and picked it up. He stood on the far side of the office, hefting the book reflectively, lips pursed as he looked at Patterson.

'He'll do it, you know, sir,' he said.

'He's a vengeful bastard.'

'I know, I know,' Patterson grumbled. 'I just hate the smarmy bastard, that's all. Is he queer, do you think?'

'I don't know,' Christie said impatiently. 'What difference does it make?'

'I might put him under surveillance for a couple of weeks,' Patterson mused. 'See what turns up.'

'For God's sake, major, don't even think such things!' Christie said, aghast. 'There'd be all hell to pay.'

'All right, all right, give him the damned dossier!' Patterson said. 'But not until one minute to four, understand?'

Christie sighed. He sometimes wondered whether he didn't prefer the war going on outside. It was just as dirty, but at least you knew who the enemy were.

4

Clive Bradley was as well aware of what had happened to Maurice Abernethy as the rest of the DI5 couriers at Curzon Street House. Like them, he had seen the telecast pictures of the smoking, twisted heap of scrap metal in which Abernethy had died; and, like them, he had wondered why anyone would want so spectacularly to destroy so harmless a man. It had said on the newscast that the IRA claimed responsibility, but not why they had chosen Abernethy as a target. He had apparently not been carrying material with a particularly high security classification. Of course, it might well be that the security services were controlling what the media told the public. It certainly wouldn't be the first time. Damage limitation, they called it.

Even though Clive Bradley had known Abernethy only slightly, his death seemed a pointless waste. But then, so did every death in Northern Ireland, whether it was a young soldier or an innocent child. Bradley had no patience with those who advocated a British withdrawal. Leaving the country to be consumed by civil war was no more the answer than taking out every known terrorist, putting him up against a wall and shooting him. Although there were one or two countries in the world where they would have done just that, he thought.

The British Airways stewardess was bending over one of the passengers, answering his questions. Bradley's eyes followed the lissom movement of her body beneath the uniform blouse. She was an attractive blonde girl with a knowing, saucy smile that attracted him, and a Liverpool accent that she took no trouble at all to conceal. He knew from the badge on her jacket that her name was Lynn. If this had been anything other than a Super Shuttle, he would have invited her to have dinner with him, but he knew cabin crew on the Belfast run only did night stops if they were taking the last flight over.

He disembarked in a haze of apathy and followed the BA courier through the diplomatic channel to the waiting car. The security check was perfunctory; on the far side of the security corridor, two armed military motorcyclists kicked their machines into roaring action and moved out ahead of them on to the Temple-patrick road.

The road ran straight as a ruled line for two and a half miles. Off to the right was a low hill. A sign flashed by: Ballyrobin. They whisked through a small hamlet of white-painted houses. Up ahead was the bridge that carried the old Belfast-Antrim road, beyond it the hamlet of Clady Bridge. As they flashed beneath it, the motorcycle escort, perhaps four yards ahead of the car, tripped the mine beneath the culvert under the road across Clady Water.

The sergeant driving had no chance at all. The enormous explosive blast lifted the car off the ground and flipped it over like a child's toy, its engine still roaring as it landed on its roof and skidded sideways with a smashing, ugly, metallic sound into the gaping, burning hole that had been torn in the road, then came to rest nose down, steam seething from the burst radiator. The pattering rain of earth and gravel and softer, wetter things stopped; smoke rose in a turning spiral. One of the motorcycles, twisted almost beyond recognition, lay beside the smoking crater in the middle of the road, a wheel turning, slower and slower. The two escorts had disappeared completely.

The driver was not dead. His movements slow and weary, like those of an exhausted swimmer, he managed to kick out what was left of the windscreen. He was trying to squirm out of the crushed body of the car when a man wearing a black sweater and slacks, his head concealed in a black ski mask, ran out of hiding. He put the muzzle of a Browning automatic against the helpless soldier's temple, and pulled the trigger.

At the same time another man, dressed identically, ran out of concealment to join him. In his hand he carried a long-handled axe, the kind normally used for splitting logs. He stood the axe against the side of the car and hauled on the rear passenger door, kicking at the battered bodywork and cursing until it opened with a protesting metallic squeal. Clive Bradley's body lolled out, his mouth hanging slackly open, his scalp matted with dark, almost black blood.

'The case!' the masked man panted. 'Get the briefcase!'

The first terrorist pulled out the briefcase, which was handcuffed to Bradley's right wrist. He stood back, warily watching the road from the airport. The second man lifted the axe high and brought it down. Clive Bradley's eyes opened wide. A ghastly sound, somewhere between a scream and a groan, escaped his lips.

'Mother of God!' the first man shouted. 'He's still alive!'

The second man snatched up the blood-spattered briefcase and they ran up the road to where a blue car stood waiting, motor running. They piled into the car and the driver accelerated making a skidding right turn into the minor road going east toward Lyle Hill and the mountains ringing Belfast. By the time the Army reached the scene of the bombing and the helicopters were in the air, the three terrorists were already on their way, in separate cars, to New-townabbey.

★   ★   ★

The egg yolks, lemon juice and mustard had emulsified perfectly; Garrett now began to add the oil drop by drop, slowly at first, then more quickly. When the mayonnaise was ready he emptied it out of the food processor into a small dish and put it in the refrigerator.

'Another glass?'

'What are we eating?' Jessica said, holding out her glass. He poured more champagne for each of them.

'Poached salmon steaks, new potatoes, *mange touts*,' he said.

'With fresh mayonnaise.'

'Is there any other kind?'

'What about salmonella?'

'Free-range eggs,' he said. 'No chance.'

To accompany the fish, Garrett had

chosen an '83 Meursault from Pierre Morey. Working southwards, Meursault is one of the first of the great Burgundy white wine villages, and Morey, to Garrett's mind, one of its best vintners. They ate at the old oak table in the dining bay by the window overlooking the Thames. Garrett's flat at Whitehall Court was, he always thought, one of the better perks of his job. It contained a study, a comfortably furnished living room and dining room, two bedrooms, and a bathroom that looked as if it had been fitted out by Charles Ritz. It gave Garrett perverse pleasure to be living in the very building in which, eighty years earlier, the British secret service had been born.

Mansfield Cumming, the monocled ex-Naval officer who used to drive his Rolls-Royce through the streets of London at breakneck speeds 'to the terror of police and pedestrians alike', and went on spying expeditions in outlandish disguises, armed with only a swordstick, had lived in a top-floor flat at number two, accessible only by private lift. There, in a regular maze of passages and steps and oddly shaped rooms, he had set up the Secret Service Bureau, later MI-1c and later still the Secret Intelligence Service.

'What's for pudding?' Jessica wanted to know.

'I cheated,' Garrett confessed. 'I bought blueberries at Harrods.'

'Dock ten brownie points,' she told him. 'And bring on the blueberries.'

It was two weeks since they had come back from Greece. Jessica had flown home alone while Garrett remained in Athens to clear up his involvement in the killing of the terrorists. He learned from ESA, the Greek military police, that the six men had mounted the hijack in an attempt to effect the release of three Palestinians imprisoned in the national penitentiary near Athens. One man's terrorist is another man's patriot.

The intervening two weeks had been hectic, and this was the first time Garrett and Jessica had been able to spend an uninterrupted evening together. Jessica, he noticed, had made no mention at all of what happened on board the *Aphrodite*. They stacked the dishes in the dishwasher and took their coffee into the living room. He put a Charlie Byrd album on and sat beside Jessica on the big sofa in front of the fireplace over which hung a painting by Sir James Lavery.

'I like that painting,' Jessica said, as Charlie Byrd segued into 'My Funny Valentine'. 'Your father gave it to you, didn't he?'

'Correct.'

'What's he like?'

'My father? Like me. Only older. Why don't you come out to Homefield and meet him?'

'One of these days,' Jessica said. 'I'm not sure I'm ready for your family yet.'

'You'd like them, Jess,' he told her. 'I know they'd like you.'

'I'm just an ordinary girl, Charles,' she said. 'I grew up in a five-bed detached in Finchley, not a stately home.'

'It's not a stately home,' he protested. 'It's a sandstone pile. Twenty-eight rooms, half of which are closed down most of the year.'

'With a hundred and fifty acres,' she pointed out.

Garrett grinned. 'What's all this sudden interest in my family?'

'I'm trying to put you into some kind of context,' Jessica said, getting up and walking across to the window. The lights on the South Bank were bright against the indigo evening sky.

'I was hoping you'd lead the way.'

He shrugged.

'It's a long story.'

'I'm not in a hurry,' she said, folding her legs under her on the sofa and leaning back. 'Take your time.'

'Once upon a time, before there was Israel, there was Palestine. Britain freed it from the Turks during World War One, and became a sort of occupying power. We kept the peace there — more or less — until the end of World War Two, when Jewish immigration began in earnest. I knew my father had served in Palestine. I knew he'd been wounded during a roundup of terrorists in Jerusalem, but not the details. Then one day I asked him about it, and he told me all about the Irgun.'

'What was the Irgun?'

'More history,' he warned her. The Jews of Palestine were not allowed to bear arms until World War Two, he went on, when an eccentric British military genius named Orde Wingate created a crack fighting unit, Palmach, which grew into Haganah, the first Jewish military organization. At the end of the war, as Jewish militancy mounted, a splinter group of Haganah joined another organization led by a man named Jabotinsky to form Irgun Zvai Leumi; other paramilitary groups sprang up. They conducted a guerilla war against the British; their most famous attacks were the bombing of the King David Hotel in Jerusalem, and the destruction of twenty-two RAF planes on the ground at Kastina airport.

It was during a roundup of suspects following the hotel bombing that George Garrett, then a major in the Royal Signals, was cut down by a young Israeli using a Sten gun that shattered both the young English officer's legs.

'It was a couple of years before he could walk properly again,' Garrett continued. 'The astonishing thing was, he never held a grudge against the people who had crippled him. He said you had to look at it from their point of view as well. They believed as fiercely in what they were doing as the British. You could never hope to fight them successfully if you didn't understand that.'

'When did he tell you all this?'

'On my fourteenth birthday. He gave me an old shotgun and took me on a rough shoot, looking for pigeon or rabbits. While we walked, he told me about Palestine. And I thought, I'll find out more about that. I read some books, but they didn't really tell me anything. Palestine was a bit of a backwater in World War Two. It wasn't until I went to Oxford that I started studying the subject properly. After that, it was a bit like Topsy: it just growed. I did my master's dissertation on how the KGB manipulates terrorists as part of its destabilization techniques. The lookouts read it and offered me a job.'

'Lookouts?'

'The security services have people at all the universities, Jess. They call themselves civil service recruitment officers, but they're really talent spotters. I was obviously what they were looking for.'

'So you joined the secret service?'

'It's never quite that cut and dried, but yes. I went to Foreign and Common-wealth first, of course. They gave me three months' training at Curzon, followed by a month at the SIS training school in Borough High Street and a week at the field centre at Fort Monkton.'

'That's at Portsmouth.'

'Gosport,' he said. 'They teach you how to get out of places you shouldn't have gone to in the first place. You sure you're interested in all this?'

'Do they teach you . . . the things you did on that ship in Greece?'

'Ah,' he said. 'I wondered when you'd ask about that.'

'I saw you kill four men. Like a machine.'

'That's what they teach you,' he said. 'To close out everything else. To concen-trate on the one thing you need to do next.'

'Who is *they*?'

'Every country in the world has an élite force, Jess. Here in England it's the SAS. The 22nd Special Air Services regiment, based at Stirling Lines, near Hereford.'

'I know who the SAS are, Charles. They were the ones who ended the siege at the Iranian Embassy in 1980.'

'That was Pagoda troop. The people who trained me at Hereford. I was there for six weeks.'

The training was intensive and comprehensive, he told her. They showed him how to use the computer banks, with comprehensive data — down to the thickness of walls and doors, the composition of floors — on likely terrorist targets such as embassies, airports and government buildings. He also became familiar with the 'Spies' system, by means of which the computers could create a holographic replica of a building, to which the images of the terrorists and their locations had been added, then 'walk' the team through it plotting lines of fire.

After that, they began a punishing three-week regimen of physical training that included survival techniques, HALO — high altitude, low opening — parachute jumps, and a series of safe-or-dead solo sorties that culminated in a forty-mile forced march, with full fifty-five-pound Bergen pack and rifle, through the Welsh mountains. Then came what was known as 'R to I' — resistance to interrogation — the session most of the men dreaded. For up to thirty-six hours, each man was deprived of sleep and held naked, in darkness, between interrogation sessions. The questioners — sometimes they were women — used both 'soft' and 'hard' techniques which ranged from physical abuse to disparaging remarks about the size of a man's sexual organs. The only reply permitted was 'I cannot answer that question.' Only when he had passed this test was Garrett — or anyone else — allowed to participate in an 'operation'.

Off near the northwestern perimeter was an unlit building they called 'the killing house', specially constructed so that SAS squads could practise rescue and termination techniques. In mock sieges and hostage rescues, in hijack simulations carried out in the model of a Boeing 747 concealed from the outside world inside a pitch-black hangar, Garrett learned the rules the hard way. Only live ammunition was used. If anyone made a mistake, somebody got killed.

Inside the rambling, unlit house was 'the killing room', a cramped and lethal dead zone; the instructors gave each team no more than four seconds to clear and secure it. Sweating in a fire-retardant suit overlaid with bulletproof jacket and ceramic composite plates, head encased in a ballistic composite helmet with ear protection and communications headset, respirator incorporating microphone, night-vision goggles, and combat boots, Garrett led or acted as backup in four such exercises a day every day for two weeks. Every single day he fired over a thousand rounds of ammunition from the Heckler & Koch MP5 submachine gun with which he had been issued.

'You learn to concentrate so com-pletely, so utterly, that there are no other people in the world except you and the enemy. Everything else is . . . out there. Not *in here*.'

'And when it's over?'

'It's like awakening from a very vivid dream. You can remember everything that happened very clearly, but there is an air of unreality about it. As if what you did, you did in some other plane of existence.'

'It's still killing, Charles.'

'I wasn't trying to justify it, Jess. Just explain it.'

'You did all that in six weeks?'

'They were only teaching me the essentials,' he told her. 'A regular soldier trains for up to two years, and even then he may be RTU — returned to his unit, not accepted by the regiment. Only about fifteen out of every hundred make it.'

'I'm not surprised,' Jessica said. 'Is it still the same?'

'There's a new system now. The SAS, Territorial SAS, the Special Boat Service and the Intelligence and Security Group — the one I was attached to — were brought together in 1988 under a Director of Special Forces based at the Ministry of Defence.'

'And he decides who does what.'

'Pretty much. It's all very hush-hush. A full squadron is always on call for special projects. It is known as CRWU, the counter-revolutionary warfare unit. They carry out counter-terrorist operations outside the United Kingdom.'

'Like Gibraltar?'

'Like Gibraltar,' he agreed gravely. 'Or direct confrontations with the IRA in Northern Ireland.'

'I thought DI5 and DI6 handled Northern Ireland?'

'Five and Six are covert, not overt, Jess,' he explained. 'Their main activity is to watch people. There's only one organization which is allowed to zap bandits.'

'And get away with it.'

'That's the moral issue, isn't it?' Garrett said. 'Is it right to kill a terrorist before he can kill innocent people?'

'Well, is it?'

'Nobody knows,' he said. 'You just do what you're sent to do.'

'Doesn't that make you a sort of state executioner?'

'A wounded terrorist with a transceiver can still set off a bomb that will kill a hundred people and maim twice that many again,' he said. 'You don't dare take the chance.'

'So the motto is, take no prisoners.'

'You've seen it in action,' he reminded her.

'I remember.' She shivered slightly and moved closer to him.

'How did we get on to this topic?'

'It's my fault,' she said. 'I keep trying to understand you.'

'How are you doing?'

'Not very well,' she confessed. 'You're very complex, and that's what intrigues me. I could understand your doing what you do if you came from a different background. If you'd spent two years with the SAS instead of two months. But you were trained as a diplomat, not a blunt instrument.'

'I'm a bit of both,' Garrett said. 'It all depends on the circumstances. In Greece, there was no opportunity to use diplomacy.'

'Would you have done so if there was?'

'You think I enjoyed doing what I did?'

'I don't know,' she said thoughtfully. 'Did you?'

'We've had this conversation before,' he said doggedly. 'What about a liqueur?'

'Ah,' Jessica said. 'Change the subject, Jessica.'

'What do you want to know, Jess?' he asked her. 'What exactly is it you're trying to ask me?'

'I don't know. How you live with it, I suppose. How you come to terms with it.'

'I think of you.'

'Me?'

'Yes, you. I think of you, getting up in the morning, having breakfast, going to work, coming home. I think of you brushing your hair, buying a dress, sipping a glass of wine, doing whatever you want to do. And I know whatever I have to do to make it possible for you and all the other people like you in the world to go on living your life without fear, it's worth it.'

'That's a good answer, Charles,' she said softly.

5

Garrett took a cab up to Berkeley Square and told the driver to stop on the corner of Hill Street. He walked around the top of the square — the gardens were closed at this time of night — to the narrow mews that ran alongside Lonsdale House parallel to Bruton Street. Inserting his keycard in the slot by the night-duty door, he punched in his security number on the numerical keyboard. After a moment the deadlocks clacked open and a fit-looking young man in a dark suit which did not quite conceal the discreet bulge of the shoulder holster beneath his left arm held the door open.

'Evenin', sir,' he said.

He led the way across to the duty desk, where Garrett pressed his thumb on to a small square of frosted glass set into the counter and waited while the scanner fed it into the computer. After a moment the unit emitted a sharp ping not unlike a microwave oven. The young security officer smiled. He knew perfectly well who Garrett was, of course; but nobody, and that meant nobody, was admitted to this building without the thumbprint check.

'Director's expecting you, sir,' he said. 'Take the second lift, please.'

The lift that took Garrett to the third floor — there were no stairs — debouched into an open parqueted hallway with a semicircular desk at the far side. A plain brass plaque on the wall bore the simple legend 'Diversified Corporate Facilities, Ltd'. Legend was the correct word: DFC was a simple front for the secret organization of which Charles Garrett was a senior executive.

Doors to the right and left of the desk led to a brightly lit inner foyer; in spite of the lateness of the hour, the soft mutter of electronic machinery could be heard. At the desk, Garrett again provided the scanner with a thumbprint and waited for the bleep. Like his colleague on the ground floor, the security officer on this level knew who Garrett was; but exceptions to the clearance drill were not countenanced.

'Right-hand door, Mr Garrett,' the man said, and pressed the button beneath his desk which released the locks. Garrett went through to the inner foyer, which also doubled as a waiting room. To his right and left were the doors which led into the north and south aisles; on the former were the finance and administration offices and the library, while the latter was the home of Registry, Computers, and the five executive offices, one of which was his own. Directly ahead was a third, unmarked door which led into a grey-carpeted corridor with double doors at its end. Garrett walked to the doors, positioned himself on the marked square set into the carpeting so that the CCTV camera could log his entry, then pushed the buzzer.

The electronic locks opened almost at once, and as he went through into Liz James' office, he heard Bleke playing the harmonium. Bach, he thought; well, more or less, anyway. He grinned in the darkness. Normally Bleke's secretary's office was brightly lit, but Liz would have left at seven as usual. One of the two doors leading into Bleke's office stood open, throwing a bright shaft of light across the floor.

'Come in, Charles,' he heard Bleke call. 'Come in.'

He was sitting at the harmonium, his feet working the pump pedals as he played, head back, eyes closed. What was it now? Garrett wondered. One of the fugues? The Old Man's keyboard technique was a well-worn joke at Lonsdale House. There was said to be reward on offer to anyone who could find Bleke's music teacher — and kill him before he could teach anyone else.

The music came to its crescendo and finale, and Bleke got up and came over to the desk.

'Belfast,' he said. He left a little silence after the word. Garrett waited. 'How would you feel about going back?'

'Not ecstatic,' Garrett said.

'I can understand that,' Bleke nodded. 'I wouldn't even suggest it if I could think

71

of an alternative.'

He was a short, stockily built man with shrewd, alert eyes, a firm mouth and resolute jaw. He wore a Gieves & Hawkes suit, well tailored but very conservatively cut, with a Turnbull & Asser silk shirt and discreet tie.

'What's the problem?' Garrett asked.

By way of answering the question, Bleke pushed a dossier across the desk; Garrett noted the diagonal red stripe that indicated it was highly restricted. He turned it round. The computer-generated classification tag read SOPAR-8/ASSREP-HENNESSY. Any acronym ending -PAR indicated third-level security rating; there were fifteen classifications in all, followed by further 'soft' codings. The number following the acronym meant that only eight copies of the secret document had been raised. ASSREP was simple spookspeak for 'assessment report' and what followed was the name of or alloted to the subject of the assessment.

'Hennessy,' Garrett said softly. 'He's back in business, then?'

Bleke nodded. 'Something new,

Charles,' he said. 'Something nasty. An assassination unit.'

'An assassination squad sanctioned by the IRA?'

'I doubt they could be operating otherwise. Although we are considering the possibility of a mad-dog operation.'

'What were the couriers carrying?'

'Five is being a bit tight-lipped about it,' Bleke replied. 'Abernethy's consignment was nonsensitive, but I understand the second man was carrying gold. A complete DI5 assessment of KGB penetration of the IRA.'

'And Hennessy's group has it?'

'They took it off the body. With an axe.' Bleke pushed a folder of scene-of-crime photographs across. Garrett looked at them dispassionately. They were not pretty.

'What's our interest?' he asked. 'Can't DI5 or military intelligence handle it themselves?'

'They're in a mess, Charles,' Bleke said. 'I talked to Patrick Walker only a couple of hours ago.' Walker was Director General of DI5, the domestic security service based in Curzon Street House.

'And?'

'He told me his man in Lisburn has threatened to quit unless they do something about the madman running MI. Absolute shambles, he says. Apparently the fellow beat a suspect to death a few days ago. It's been whitewashed, of course, but that doesn't alter the facts. The man won't listen, won't co-operate. Apparently he's known on the street as Qhaddafi. Qhaddafi, for God's sake! Five says if he isn't controlled, there'll be a bloodbath.'

'I don't see the problem,' Garrett said. 'If he's as bad as Five say, all the ministry has to do is yank him out and replace him.'

'Thought you'd say that. Exactly my feelings. So I had a word with Sir Edward at the ministry. He told me the facts are the very opposite of what Five represents them to be. He says his people are complaining that DI5 is seriously undermining the undercover activities of military intelligence, and that if they're not brought to heel, MI will come to a grinding halt.'

"'No one is such a liar as the indignant man.'"

He saw that Bleke was staring at him uncomprehendingly. 'Nietzsche,' he said. 'Sorry. This Qhaddafi. Who is he?'

'Chap called Harry Patterson. Major, Signals. Do you know him?'

'The name rings a faint bell,' Garrett said, frowning as he tried to put a face to the name. 'I'll check him on the magic box. What about Five's man?'

'Stephen Elkins,' Bleke said.

Garrett nodded. 'Him I know,' he said. Smooth Steve had been his 'classmate' at the escape and evasion school in Gosport. Garrett remembered Elkins as one of those lard-bodied, ungainly men, hopeless at anything requiring physical co-ordination. Elkins had become the butt of the bluntly spoken NCOs whose job it was to drill in the use of weapons and the negotiation of electrified fences and booby-trapped walls.

The name of the firearms sergeant instructor was Hanley. Everybody called him Tommy. He looked like all the gym teachers Garrett had ever seen. He brought out a wooden orange crate and from it produced a Browning 9 mm automatic and a magazine of ammunition for each of them.

'Wot you 'ave in your 'ot little 'ands, my gentlemen, is a hoffensive weapon,' he shouted, with leaden good humour. 'I shall now hendeavour to show you 'ow to use it.'

For three-quarters of an hour he made them practise: slap the empty magazine into the butt of the gun, slip off the safety, fall automatically into the approved two-handed crouch, and dry-fire at the plywood target. Three-quarters of an hour in a whipping wind that came edge-on through the naked trees on the cliffs above Stokes Bay, slicing through their MoD-issue pullovers as if they were made of paper. By the time they actually came to fire the guns, their hands and feet were numb with cold, and the sergeant instructor in his baggy training suit and rosy-apple cheeks could have cooked a meal on the glow of their antipathy.

Elkins was the dunce of the class. The gun bucked in his hands like a rabbit held by the heels, and the S/I looked at him ruefully, shaking his head and pursing his lips like a ham actor.

'Dear oh dear oh dearie me,' he said heavily. 'You're 'oldin' that gun like a young virgin 'oldin' 'er first dick, my gentleman. Never do, that won't. So I'll say to you wot I'd say to 'er — get 'old of it proper if you want to enjoy it!'

He got his laugh. Elkins gritted his teeth and banged away another magazine, hatred simmering in his eyes. Finally, the S/I called it a day. He reeled in Elkins' target and showed it to him. There were three holes in it; Elkins had fired perhaps four nine-round magazines.

'Well, my gentleman,' the S/I said cheerfully. 'Just 'ave to 'ope you never meet the bloody enemy, won't we?'

He turned away to get the wooden box to put the guns back into. As he turned, Elkins levelled the automatic at the sergeant's back and pulled the trigger.

'Bang,' he said, as the hammer clicked on the empty gun. Hanley whirled round, his eyes slitted with disbelief and, perhaps, fear.

'You fuckin' lunatic!' he shouted, his

voice cracking. 'What you fuckin' think you're doin'?'

Elkins smiled blandly. 'Giving you your first lesson in intelligence work, you detestable little creep,' he said. 'Know thine enemy.'

He threw the Browning at the sergeant's feet and strode away; if the instructor ever took any disciplinary action, none of them ever heard about it. Maybe he did and it got buried in someone's NAN — no action now — file. Elkins had connections at the top. A long time ago, Garrett thought; he shook his head slightly to clear away the cobwebs of memory, and stood up.

'Take the dossier,' Bleke told him. 'It won't tell you much more than I did. I'd like you to get over to Belfast as soon as you can. See what you can do to sort this mess out.'

'I'll start now,' Garrett said. 'If I can get the ground-work done tonight, I can leave for Belfast on Tuesday morning.'

'Talk to Arthur Cotton,' Bleke said. 'Tell him I said to give you a first-class ticket.'

'There's no first class on the shuttle, sir,' Garrett pointed out.

'Oh,' Bleke said, with a smile that said he had known that all along.

★   ★   ★

Garrett took the dossier and went to his office, a functional suite at the far end of the north aisle, with a big window looking out across Berkeley Square. The streets outside were silent and empty; it was already after midnight. He thought of Jessica asleep in his bed at the flat; maybe if he got finished in time, they could have breakfast together.

For the next hour he punched in questions, routing them via R2, the security service mainframe at Euston Tower, which in turn passed them to the TREVI computer network in Europe. On this were stored the combined anti-terrorist records of all the NATO countries. Garrett always thought that the French bureaucrat who had created the name of the organization must have been a James Bond fan: the acronym TREVI stood for *Terrour, Radicalisme et Violence Internationale*.

One by one he directed his enquiries to the participating countries: France, Germany, Belgium, Holland and the rest. The average citizen had no conception of the speed at which such computers could work. The TREVI main-frame could transfer the contents of five thousand books of three hundred pages each in a second, producing hard copy at one hundred thousand lines a minute. Capable of handling upwards of two million flops — calculations — a second, such a machine was perhaps fifty or sixty thousand times faster than the fastest business computer currently in use.

The results of his trawl started coming in about twenty minutes later: France, NKTO, Belgium, NKTO, Holland, NKTO — nothing known to this organization. He left the computers to carry on without him, and turned to something else. He keyed in the codes for registry search, added the appropriate name and references, and watched as the screen filled with the service history of Major John

Harold Patterson, head of military intelligence at Northern Ireland Security Service Headquarters.

Garrett keyed rapidly through the vital statistics: oldest son of James and Hilda (Higgins) Patterson, born in Manchester exactly one year after the outbreak of World War Two. Scholarship to the famed Bluecoat School, and from there to Manchester University, where he graduated with a good arts degree. Joined the Army in 1964; commissioned a second lieutenant in the Royal Corps of Signals. Served in Malaysia and Borneo; cleared on unspecified charges of brutality to prisoners in 1969, he transferred to the Intelligence Corps. Next six years Oman. Two more disciplinary hearings: again both to do with maltreatment of prisoners. No action taken; allegations not sustained, proceedings before a courtmartial therefore unnecessary. In the same period, Patterson rose from the rank of captain to major. Active service in the Falklands War; during this conflict he got the nickname 'Qhaddafi' because of his bombastic boastfulness and reckless disregard for life — his own or anyone else's. Posted to NISSHQ as junior liaison officer, military intelligence; assumed command late in 1987.

'All very interesting,' Garrett grunted. 'Let's move on to the PA report.'

The psychological assessment had been carried out over a three-day period at Kelvin House, the Central Medical Establishment of the Ministry of Defence. Garrett read it carefully, making notes on a feint-ruled notepad. Couched in the careful 'psychologese' of the Kelvin headshrinkers, it told him that Major Harry Patterson, head of British military intelligence in Northern Ireland, was a martinet, a bully and a woman-hater; well, there were plenty of those in every Army in the world.

The returns were still coming in from TREVI; it looked as though he was going to draw a blank on Hennessy's new associates, whoever they were, wherever he had found them. The cursor was blinking yet again alongside the acronym NKTO — nothing known to this organization — which meant that the *Bundesamt für Verfassungsschutz*, the

Office for the Protection of the Constitution in Cologne, Germany's equivalent of DI5, knew nothing about them either. He was not sanguine about the Italians or Greeks coming up with anything.

He went back to the small PC console and punched in another set of codes, this time conjuring up the service record of Stephen Benton Elkins. The man might have been born to go into the security service, Garrett thought as he scanned the dossier: third son of Sir Harold and Lady Pamela (Horrocks) Elkins of Tenterden, Kent, Educated at Eton and then Fettes, he went straight into the Foreign Office for a year; he was inducted into intelligence by a selection board on the fifth floor of MI5's former headquarters, a building with teak-inlaid corridors and corniced offices opposite the White Elephant Club on Curzon Street.

He started off in A2, then got shunted into F, which was a mess, run by a well-meaning drunk. His greatest moment came when he led the team which unmasked Peter Jordan, a retired sixty-one-year-old schoolteacher who was an intelligence gatherer for the Irish National Liberation Army. Over two years, Jordan had compiled extensive dossiers on three senior generals, the heads of both DI5 and DI6, and a senior judge, setting them up as possible targets. Subsequent to this coup, Elkins had been promoted to senior liaison officer for Five at NIHQ. His record there had been less than spectacular.

'Lucky Jim,' Garrett said aloud. Elkins had been in the right places at the right time; his father, who was a senior assistant to the coordinator of intelligence for the joint chiefs, had seen to the rest. You didn't need a qualification in psychology to realize how badly someone like Harry Patterson would react to a man like Elkins.

'Let's have a look at your psy-profile, Steven,' Garrett murmured. He punched in the code and poured himself another cup of coffee while the computer produced the information. The machine hummed and buzzed; the screen filled with information like a cistern filling with water. Most of it was as predictable as

Miami weather. Elkins believed his enormous conceit to be nothing more than a perfectly acceptable satisfaction with his own abilities, and his intolerance completely justified by the fact that most of the people he had to deal with were his intellectual as well as social inferiors.

'When questioned about his personal life,' the report went on, 'this officer seemed to find the matter tiresome, his attitude clearly indicating that no one on the examining board was qualified socially to make a judgement. It is considered that this officer's propensity for extramarital activities might make him a target for blackmail; his superiors are enjoined to ensure he is never posted to a location where he might be placed in such jeopardy.'

Garrett permitted himself a thin smile; Elkins would find few enough temptations in Ulster. Which, if the report was anything to go on, was probably just as well. He wondered what Fiona Elkins was like. The records indicated that she was the daughter of the Honourable Cyril Jamison, a former debutante, amateur showjumper and horse breeder, now thirty-eight. Mrs Elkins had not gone to Ireland with her husband;

Garrett went across to the IBM again; all the TREVI reports were in now, and as he had expected, the result was nil. Hennessy's assassination squad were new boys, or old hands masquerading under a new name. At the outset, such a group had everything on their side; in the war of the flea the dog had to wait until it was bitten. After a while, though, unlike the flea, the terrorist left a shadow, then a blurred image, and eventually a picture.

Right now, however, all Garrett had was the fact that Hennessy and his killers had assassinated two DI5 couriers. The overt evidence seemed to indicate that the papers Abernethy and Bradley had been carrying might be the motive, but there was something about the way Hennessy had announced his participation, as if the boast was a challenge, that made Garrett wonder if there was something else behind the killings.

Why had Hennessy gone back to Ulster? How had he managed to get out of Germany and back into Ireland? Was he acting with IRA backing, tacit or otherwise, or was he a wild card? Why had he embarked upon this campaign of murderous overkill? Why DI5 couriers? Was this the beginning of a campaign of assassinations, or were these simply what the terrorists called 'targets of opportunity'? How and where had the killers got the information that enabled them to lay such murderously successful ambushes? Garrett shook his head: if there were answers to his questions, there was only one place to find them. He picked up the phone to leave a message for Arthur Cotton, who handled transportation.

Belfast.

There were a lot of ghosts there.

6

Memories always sneaked up on you just when you least wanted them around, Garrett thought. As the plane banked to port over the slate-grey sea below, his mind went back to the first time his wife Diana had come to Belfast.

Christ, what an awful place, Diana said. It's as if whoever built these houses hated the people who were going to live in them.

They were driving through the suburbs of Belfast. It was a grey Tuesday afternoon in December and a thin drizzle had begun to fall. Pedestrians hurried along in the glistening streets, heads down against the unfriendly wind.

Don't worry, he told her. We won't be living up in this part of town. He tried to make a joke of it, but Diana was in no mood for humour.

I'm going to hate it, Charles, she said. I'm sorry but I am definitely going to hate it here.

Give it a chance, he said. There are
some beautiful places nearby. Bangor.
The Mountains of Mourne —

Mountains! she said scornfully. They're
not even three thousand feet high.

That's high, he grinned. For Ireland.

I wish we were back in Berlin. I was
having such a good time there.

We've only been here a week. When we
get to know a few people it will be
different.

She shook her head. Look at them, she
said, with an angry gesture at the people
in the streets. Why do they look so
damned . . . dejected?

She was right about one thing, he
thought. She said she was going to hate it,
and she hated it. From the first day until
the last, she hated the place and she hated
the people. When she died, they asked
him where he wanted her buried. It was
something you never thought about until
it was too late to ask. He knew she would
not want it to be in Ireland. Much, much
later, he had flown to Berlin, rented a
small plane and sprinkled her ashes over
the city she had always loved best. They

told him it was illegal; he told them to go to hell.

He took a taxi into town; it was no guarantee that his arrival would not be logged, but if he was met by an official car, the IRA watchers at the airport would take considerably more notice. The trip into town was uneventful; since he knew he would not be staying, he checked in at the Europa. As soon as he had hung up his clothes and made a few telephone calls, he left the hotel and took a walk through the pedestrianized centre of town; it was pretty much the same as he remembered it.

Armed soldiers manned a dozen checkpoints surrounding an area of about a mile square, through which all vehicles had to pass. No vehicle was allowed through without a passenger, and no parking was permitted in the centre without a special pass. The Royal Ulster Constabulary carried out random checks on all buses. Taxis were banned from the enclave because their two-way radios might trigger off bombs. It was like a city in wartime, yet for all that the streets were crowded with shoppers; in spite of the bombs and the terrorism, life somehow went on.

Garrett walked back down Queen Victoria Street and went into the Crown. It was no ordinary pub: the Crown Liquor Saloon was a tourist's dream of an Irish pub, with an interior so ornately Victorian baroque that it was almost a travesty, a riot of marble-topped bar, lavishly decorated mirrors, gingerbread woodwork, mosaic-tile floors and brass-ware. There were nickel plates for striking matches and an elaborate system of numbered bells above each snug, or booth, with corresponding letters on the bell board across the centre of the bar. A sign advised patrons that — unlike the youth of England — persons under twenty-one years of age would not be served.

It was the kind of place Garrett would normally have avoided like the plague even though, at this time of day and this time of year, there were only a few people in it. He ordered a half-pint of draught Guinness at the bar and took it over into one of the booths, opening his copy of the

Independent at the sports pages.

'If that's Guinness you're drinkin', I'll have one of the same,' a soft voice said. Garrett put down the paper. A small, thin-lipped, narrow-jawed man with thoughtful green eyes had slid into the booth and was sitting opposite him. He wore a grey felt trilby hat and a black overcoat with lapels that had gone out of style in the fifties.

'Well, well, if it isn't Danny Flynn,' Garrett said. 'And still wearing that bloody old coat.'

'Make that a pint, would you?' Flynn said. 'Seein' it's me first today.'

Garrett went across to the bar for the drinks. Flynn picked up Garrett's paper and was scanning the racing form when he brought them back.

'Dandy Dick in the three-fifteen at Wexford,' he said, tapping the paper with a nicotine-stained forefinger. 'A cert, he is, and at ten to one as well.'

Garrett shook his head, smiling.

'He's a cert, I tell you,' Danny said, all wounded dignity. 'Straight from the jockey, so it is.'

'I'll think about it,' Garrett said. 'How've you been, Danny?'

'Shure the world keeps turnin', and me wid it,' Flynn replied, taking a sip from the glass. The wary green eyes never stopped moving, checking every new face that came into the pub, flicking from one to another, watchful as a small animal that knows it has many natural enemies.

'You're looking well,' Garrett said. 'Are you still in the same . . . business?'

'In a manner of speaking,' Danny said, looking around. Nobody was taking any notice of them. He used a little machine to roll a cigarette, then stuck it in his mouth and lit it, breaking the match with his thumb. 'And what about you, Mr Garrett? What brings you here?'

'I'm just another tourist, Danny,' Garrett said.

Flynn grinned. 'And wasn't it you that told me all those years ago you'd never set foot in this godforsaken hellhole again as long as you lived.'

'Did I say that?'

'A long time ago, chief,' Danny replied softly.

*She started towards him. He gave
McCaffery a shove. Get moving, he told
him. Diana was looking at him strangely.
The expression on her face was defiant,
almost angry, like that of a child who
expects to be scolded but is not
repentant. He felt something turn inside
him. No, he thought, not that. Then he
looked at Hennessy. Even at this distance
he could see the contempt in the
Irishman's pale blue eyes. Yes, they said.
Yes, I had her. He felt the cold ugly rush
of hatred erupt inside him, then all in the
same moment he heard the spiteful
whiplash crack of a sniper's rifle and Pat
McCaffery's head exploded in a red mist
and —*

'Yes,' Garrett said. 'A long time ago.'
He got up, gesturing towards Danny
Flynn's empty glass. 'Another of those?'

'A half this time. Then you can tell me
what you wanted to see me for.'

Garrett put a packet of Rizla cigarette
papers on the table and went over to the
bar. Danny Flynn took the top slip out of
the pack, read the word on it, then put
the rice paper into his mouth, chewing it

reflectively. Garrett brought back the drinks and set them on the table as Danny lit another cigarette.

'I thought it might be him,' he said. 'That's why you're here.'

'That's why I'm here.'

God damn you, Garrett! We'll settle this one day!

'Ten years,' Danny said. 'You people have long memories.'

'So do they, Danny,' Garrett said. 'You of all people ought to know that.'

'He'll be well protected, chief.'

'That kind always are,' Garrett said, more harshly than he intended. 'Have you heard anything?'

'I've heard rumours.'

'What sort of rumours?'

'Just rumours. They said he was shot up. Damned near died.'

'It was in Germany,' Garrett said. 'A place called Lauenburg.'

'Ah,' Danny said softly. 'Was that you, too?'

The car slewed across the bridge over the river. Hennessy rolled out. The sharp crack of pistol fire. And there he was, a defiant figure silhouetted against the sky as he clambered on to the rail of the bridge above the purling Elbe. Garrett fired three shots, and knew at least one must have hit.

Hennessy screamed something unintelligible and then he was gone, down to the dark turning water below.

That close. That close, and still the bastard got away.

'We hear he's got a new unit,' Garrett said. 'An assassination squad.'

'Ah,' Danny said. 'Now I've got it. The Queen's Messengers.'

'Very good,' Garrett said. 'You haven't lost your touch, Danny.'

'I'd have been dead long since if I had,' Flynn replied flatly. 'And asking questions about . . . our friend won't be the easiest gig I ever played.'

'Don't take any chances,' Garrett told him sharply. 'Just keep your ears open. You know what I want.'

'I'll put out some feelers,' Danny said. 'It'll take a little palm grease, Mr Garrett.'

Garrett nodded, took a bulky nine-by-six manila envelope out of his pocket and slid it across the table.

'There's two hundred and fifty in there,' he said. 'I'll get more if you need it. Where do we meet?'

'The Palm House in the Botanical Gardens. There's a bench in front of it, by a tree. An American tree, *Sassafras albidum*.'

'A sassafras tree,' Garrett said, shaking his head and smiling. 'You're full of surprises, Danny. All right, when?'

'Tomorrow, three o'clock. No show, same time next day. And so on. Anything else?'

'You ever hear from any of our old network?'

'It's not a game for annual reunions, Mr Garrett,' Flynn observed. 'People move on, drop out. We do have a few natural deaths, you know.'

'It's good to see you again, Danny,' Garrett said. 'How's Moira?'

'Fat,' Flynn grinned. 'And happy.'

'How many kids now?'

'Four. And a bun in the oven.'

Garrett shook his head. 'Danny, how do you afford it?'

'I struggle along,' Danny replied, his eyes twinkling mischievously.

Garrett stood up and looked out of the window. The streets were slick with rain. He put on his Burberry and the battered Donegal tweed hat he always wore; Danny flynn remained where he was, his glass of Guinness only half empty.

'I'll stay and finish this,' he said. 'God hates a waster.'

'Sassafras tree,' Garrett said, shaking his head again.

He went out into the drizzle. He walked up to Howard Street then turned right into Donegall Square. The huge Victorian Gothic pile of City Hall filled the lowering sky. Buses were lined up all along the western side of the building waiting to go: to Ballyhenry, to Carnmoney, to Roughfort and Stormont and Sydenham. He got on a number 16 going to Dundonald for the four-mile ride out to Stormont. It was an unconventional way of arriving at security headquarters, but Garrett was a great believer in unconventional methods.

He paused at the entrance to the

wooded, landscaped grounds; straight ahead stood the solid Portland stone pile of the government buildings. Hidden away in a grove of trees to the east was another group of buildings, invisible from the road, housing the security services. A sign in white lettering on a red ground stood beside the unmarked path: NO ENTRY FOR UNAUTHORIZED PERSONNEL. Taking his ministry identification from his pocket, Garrett made his way down the path. Before he had gone more than a hundred yards, a young soldier in camouflage battledress grew out of the ground in front of him and to his right, 5.56 mm AR-18 Sterling Armalite levelled. Almost simultaneously, another rose from concealment just to Garrett's rear and left.

'Right!' the soldier in front of him growled. 'On the ground! Flat!'

'Before you turn me over, boys, take a look at my ID,' Garrett said, holding up the warrant. The soldier behind him came closer warily, took the card from Garrett's upheld hand and inspected it.

'What business you got 'ere?' he asked,

surlily suspicious.

'You've done your job, soldier,' Garrett replied. 'It doesn't include questioning me. You want to escort me to the gate?'

The young soldier looked at him uncertainly. Then he shrugged and shouldered his Armalite. 'Follow me, please,' he said. They walked in silence along the path between the trees for a while. Presently they reached the security enclave. A Saracen armoured personnel carrier — the locals called them 'pigs' — guarded the entrance. Eyes observed him through the observation slits. Watched by his young escort, Garrett showed his ID to the sentry. The young soldier went to an inner office and was gone several minutes. When he came back his face was expressionless.

'Major Patterson is expecting you, sir,' he said. 'I'll get someone to escort you over to the security block.'

'Just tell me where it is.'

'Sorry, sir, visitors aren't permitted to go alone.'

Garrett shrugged; he had encountered military security before, and it didn't bother him now any more than it had the last time. Nothing you could do about it. He followed his escort down a tarmac pathway through the trees to the buildings which housed Security HQ. It looked pretty much the same as it had when he had worked here.

He followed the young soldier to the stairway and up to the second floor; when they reached it, he saw that the corridor facing them was completely protected by an electronically operated steel grille. The walls were painted institutional cream. The pearl bulbs in the ceiling dome lights gave the entire place a dingy, slum-school look.

'In my day DI6, the Special Duties team, the SAS coordinator and military intelligence were all on this floor,' Garrett said conversationally, while they waited for the grille to open. 'Are they all still here?'

'Don't know, sir,' the soldier said. 'In here, please.'

He stood aside and Garrett went into a small office. The floor was covered with scuffed linoleum. A single grimy window looked out to an airshaft. Garrett sat down and picked up one of the well-used magazines on the low table. It was dated eight months earlier.

'Mr Garrett?'

He looked up to see an officer smiling at him from the doorway. He was a short, trim, handsome man with one of those moustaches that Garrett thought had gone out with David Niven; the shoulder bars indicated he was a lieutenant.

'Peter Christie,' the man said, extending a hand. 'Major Patterson's two-eye-C. Sorry to have kept you waiting.'

But not very, Garrett thought. 'No problem,' he said. 'It gave me time to appreciate the decor.'

Christie looked askance, but decided it must be a joke. 'Ah, yes,' he said, smiling. 'If you'll follow me.'

Men inside the offices flanking the corridor looked up, veiled eyes concealing their curiosity, as Garrett walked by. Christie turned a corner and went through an ante-office in which three young soldiers were working at computer consoles.

'Taking a bit of a chance, coming in that way, weren't you?' Christie said, over his shoulder.

'Was I?' Garrett asked mildly. 'Why?'

Christie stopped and stared at him. 'You London people,' he said, with a sigh of exasperation. 'You've got no idea. This way.'

Garrett allowed himself a smile as Christie led the way into an airy, light-filled room with fitted carpets and some decent furniture. Beneath the window stood a long, low cream-coloured sofa flanked by small side tables on which stood porcelain lamps; easy chairs were grouped around a low coffee table, and in the corner of the room stood a handsome walnut desk. Behind it, in a leather wing chair, sat Major Harry Patterson, his eyes unreadable behind the blue lenses of his glasses.

'Come in, Garrett,' he said. 'Take a pew. What about some coffee?'

'Coffee sounds good,' Garrett said. 'Black with one sugar, please.'

'Lay it on, Peter, there's a good fellow,' Patterson said. He leaned back in his chair and folded his hands across his middle, lifting his chin slightly to let Garrett know he could begin whenever he was ready.

'Tell me, major, do you have weak eyes?' Garrett asked.

Patterson didn't answer for a moment; Garrett's question was obviously unexpected.

'You mean the glasses? No, I wear them against glare. Gives me headaches.'

'Bad ones?'

'You didn't come here to discuss my glasses. Or my headaches.'

Garrett smiled. 'Let's talk about the headaches. I understand you have quite a few.'

'Ah,' Patterson said flatly. 'You're a comedian.'

'I was being polite, major,' Garrett said. 'Don't make the mistake of thinking that means I'm gutless.'

Patterson regarded him stonily. His voice was harsh when he spoke.

'I wouldn't bother with the tough act, if I were you. You won't be here long enough for it to matter.'

'What does that mean?'

Patterson stared at Garrett for what seemed a long time. 'Have you got any idea what we're up against here, Garrett?' he said, his voice tight with anger.

'I think so.'

'You think so, do you? Well, let me give you a few statistics. Last year we had five hundred and twenty-four shooting incidents — ten a week. We had ninety-three deaths, twenty-one of them soldiers. We had four hundred and fifty bombs, not counting the ones we defused. We — '

'I've read the statistics, major,' Garrett said. 'Get to the point.'

'Don't worry, I'll get to it,' Patterson fumed. 'It's this, Garrett. If you think I'm going to let you walk in here and take over, you've got another think coming, you and all your fucking high-powered friends in Whitehall!'

Instead of comment, Garrett slid a card across the desk. On it were a name and a telephone number. Patterson stared at it as if it were a live snake.

'What's this?'

'Sir Francis Brook is the co-ordinator

of intelligence and security for the joint chiefs,' Garrett said. 'That's his direct line. Call him and tell him what you just told me. And see what happens.'

He was quite sure of his ground; if Patterson called the co-ordinator, Sir Francis would tell him in no uncertain manner that PACT requirements took precedence over those of any other security organization.

Working in close co-operation not only with British law-enforcement and security agencies, but also with Interpol and the Europolice network TREVI, its special brief was to detect, counter and neutralize, using any means at its disposal, the planners and perpetrators of terrorist strikes and political assassinations. 'Any means' meant quite literally what it said.

Patterson was still staring at the card. He reached out and touched it with a fingertip.

'Make the call, major,' Garrett said. 'Or cut the bullshit.'

'All right,' Patterson growled grudgingly. 'What happens now?'

'Very simple,' Garrett said. 'I've been sent here to do a job. I intend to do it. You give me whatever assistance I need, whenever and wherever I need it. If you don't, you end up with your arse in a sling.'

'I take it it's OK if I don't pretend to like it?'

'Internal security,' Garrett said, ignoring the jibe. 'Is it good?'

'Watertight,' Patterson replied. 'Why?'

'Somebody got word to somebody that those couriers were coming in, perhaps even what they were carrying.'

'Nothing to do with my department. DI5 handles courier runs.'

'DI5,' Garrett said. 'That's Elkins, isn't it?'

'That proctologist,' Patterson muttered.

'I'll be talking to him, too,' Garrett said. 'In the meantime, I want you to clear me for open-ended access to your mainframe. I'll need a car — anything as long as it's not a bloody Ford — and I want your people to fix me up with a flat somewhere.'

He stood up to go. Patterson got up at

the same time, glowering at him across the desk.

'I'm not your fucking errand boy, Garrett,' he growled. 'You say please when you talk to me.'

'Of course,' Garrett said. 'Kiss my arse. Please.'

Patterson clenched his fists and lurched round the desk. When he was about halfway Garrett shook his head.

'Don't, Patterson,' he said softly. 'I'd hurt you.'

Patterson hesitated, clenching and unclenching his hands. He let his breath out slowly, and then inhaled deeply, his eyes never leaving Garrett's face. The big man waited. It was usually threats next.

'You're making a mistake antagonizing me, Garrett,' Patterson told him. 'A big mistake.'

'If there's a mistake being made, major, you're the one making it,' Garrett told him harshly. 'Now let me tell you something. Either you work with me or I'll assume you've got some reason to get in my way. If I decide that's what it is, I'll make a phone call and they'll bust you down to private and put you on street patrol in the Ardoyne.'

Patterson glowered at him for a moment longer, then shrugged. The belligerence slowly dissipated, to be replaced by a sheepish smile. Patterson gave a sort of embarrassed shrug and went behind his desk. He sat down, clasped his hands together and leaned forward.

'Well,' he said, giving it a pause that Jack Benny would have been proud of. 'Perhaps I was hasty. If so, I apologize. We get so damned many ministry people coming over here . . . you begin to get paranoid, and start thinking someone somewhere doesn't think you can do your job. But I want you to know this: you can depend on me.'

I'll bet, Garrett thought. 'I'm glad to hear it, major,' he said. 'We've got a lot to do.'

'Where would you like to start?'

'I'm going to talk to Elkins next.'

'I'll get someone to take you over — '

Garrett just smiled. Patterson frowned and then he got it.

'Ah,' he said. 'You don't want an escort.'

'I want you to feel you can trust me,' Garrett said sweetly.

'Turn right when you get out of here. Elkins is at the far end of the corridor, next to last door on your left.'

'Thanks,' Garrett said. 'I'll see you later.'

'Not if I see you first, you bastard,' Patterson said as Garrett went out the door. He thought he had said it quietly enough for the words not to carry, but Garrett heard them. He was grinning as he walked along the corridor. Garrett, you really have a way with people, he told himself.

7

'Well, well,' Elkins said. 'Charles Garrett.'

'Hello, Elkins,' Garrett said. 'Long time no see.'

Elkins' office was on a corner of the building, a second-floor suite with two large windows looking out into the parklike grounds sloping uphill to the castle.

'Sun's well below the yardarm,' Elkins said. 'Can I offer you something?'

He pressed a button somewhere on the bookcase and a portion of it slid aside, like something on a film set, revealing a small bar. He went behind it and looked up enquiringly.

'I'm told you're partial to single malts. I've a rather good Islay here.'

'You've done your homework.'

'I imagine you've done yours, too,' Elkins said, pouring the drinks. 'I hear you've been to see Qhaddafi.'

'What you might call exploratory talks,'

Garrett said, accepting a heavy crystal glass with a generous measure of Scotch in it. Elkins went behind his desk, waving Garrett to the chair opposite.

'Chin-chin,' he said, raising his glass. No wonder they called him Smooth Steve, Garrett thought. Elkins was wearing what looked like a Chester Barrie suit, handmade shoes, and a silk shirt and tie that could only have come from Jermyn Street. He had the sleek, cat-got-the-cream look of a successful ad agency account director, or one of the better-fed TV actors.

'Well, Charles, it's a long time since Gosport,' Elkins said, as if the escape and evasion centre was some kind of prep school they had attended together. 'I hear you work for Nicholas Bleke now.'

'That's right.'

'They say he's a hard man to please.'

'They tell the truth,' Garrett said. 'First things first, though. What progress have you made on Hennessy and his gang?'

Elkins picked up a dossier lying on his desk, then put it down again. He looked out of the window. He straightened his tie.

'The RUC investigation of the murder of the two couriers is still incomplete,' he said.

'Let me ask you something,' Garrett said, deciding to plunge straight in. 'Is it normal for courier cars to use a secondary road the way Abernethy did?'

'Of course not,' Elkins said sharply, as if it was a question to which any fool knew the answer. 'And Abernethy knew it. All we can surmise is that the driver suggested they'd be quicker using the B101 to Lisburn, and Abernethy went along with it. Of course, there was no way he could know the driver was a plant. They took out the real driver on his way to the airport and put their own man in our car. He set Abernethy up.'

'Nothing at the scene of the crime?'

'Clean as a whistle.'

'What about Bradley?'

'As I said, we insist that all official cars coming into Belfast use the motorway,' Elkins said. 'The roads being the way they are here, it's quicker anyway, and usually it's a hell of a lot safer. Their taking Bradley out like that caught us flatfooted. Nobody expected an attack on the car before it got on to the motorway.'

'Nothing coming in off the street?'

'We've managed to construct a generalized profile of how the cell might be constituted,' Elkins said, choosing his words carefully. 'And my people have had some success in eliminating a great many possible suspects from — '

'In other words, you haven't got anything.'

'Our investigation of the courier assassinations has led us to conclude one thing with reasonable certainty,' Elkins said. 'We've got a mole somewhere inside security headquarters.'

This was more interesting; Garrett leaned forward. 'Go on.'

'Look at the circumstances of the killings,' Elkins said. 'We have couriers coming in from London all the time. There is no predetermined pattern, no timetable, for obvious reasons of security. Yet, somehow, this gang knows that a courier will be bringing over sensitive materials of great value to the IRA, even knows it will be one of two particular couriers on one of two particular days. There's only one way they could have known everything they needed to know to do all that: by having someone on the inside.'

'He shouldn't be too difficult to isolate,' Garrett said. 'There can't be that many people who know a courier is en route.'

'Wrong,' Elkins said. 'It's common knowledge, here and at NIHQ. The schedules are circulated to every department, in case anyone has special pouch material for London.'

'Schedules, yes. But not what the couriers would be carrying.'

Elkins nodded. 'Exactly.'

'Exactly what?'

'I have positively vetted every single member of DI5 staff working here in Stormont and Lisburn,' Elkins said. 'I am prepared to state categorically that whoever and wherever this spy is, he is not in DI5.'

'Given that you're right, where do you

think he might be?'

'Good God, Charles, there are a dozen places an informant could have been infiltrated. We have no monopoly on moles and sleepers.'

'I know that,' Garrett said. 'But that's not what you started to say. You sounded as if you have some idea where he is.'

Elkins sighed, as if the admission was being forced out of him. 'All of us use field operatives and paid informants; sometimes the same ones. But one branch has more direct contact with FOs and the grasses than any other department,' Elkins said. 'And therefore, by the same token, more opportunity to pass information.'

'Military intelligence, of course,' Garrett said. 'Do you want to be more specific?'

Elkins shook his head; 'Whoever this fellow is, he's buried deep. It won't be easy to winkle him out.'

'We'll do it,' Garrett said. 'But meantime, let's get back to Hennessy. How are we going to find him, and how are we going to neutralize him?'

'I've set up a DI5 initiative,' Elkins said. 'Codename Rat Trap. This is how it will work. Curzon is sending us another courier tomorrow morning. They will advise us that he will be carrying highly sensitive material: a listing of all IRA supergrasses supplying DI5 with information on terrorist activities.'

'A surrogate?' Garrett said, surprised. 'Does the courier know what might happen to him?'

'He'll be safe enough,' Elkins said. 'You see, I'll be airside at Aldergrove when he arrives. We'll make a switch: one of my operatives is going to take his place.'

'You'll be putting your man directly in harm's way,' Garrett pointed out. 'If you're right, and Hennessy has a mole inside NIHQ, he'll tell them the courier is carrying a list of DI5 informants.'

'That's the basic idea.'

'But they might come after him in any one of half a dozen ways.'

'The difference will be that this time we'll be ready for them,' Elkins said.

'How can you be ready for them when

you don't know how they'll attack?' Garrett asked.

'I've thought of all that,' Elkins said, waving a languid hand. 'Come and take a look at the map.'

They went across to the 1:25,000-scale Ordnance Survey map of the area twenty miles around Belfast which took up most of one wall of Elkins' office.

He traced the route from Aldergrove airport with his finger. Cars leaving the arrivals building passed through a control zone, moving slowly over antispeed ramps while a battery of electronic equipment ran registration and ownership details through PDVC at Lisburn. Long before the car emerged from the security screen, everything about it and its probable occupants was known to the guards watching it go through.

Emerging from the control zone, drivers had no choice but to follow the A5 to the east-west motorway leading into Belfast. All other exit and access roads within half a mile of the airport were sealed off: the old A26 to Nutt's Corner, the Antrim road, even the lane, hardly wide enough for two cars, that ran southeast to Killead Corner. The main road ran northeast, paralleling Six Mile Water and passing through the little town of Templepatrick en route to the motorway. From there it was a clear run into Belfast.

'This time we'll outthink the bastards,' Elkins said confidently. 'The courier is coming in on BA 4572 tomorrow morning, landing at eleven-forty.' He looked at his watch. 'That's about eighteen hours from now. In the intervening period, every inch of the road between the airport and the motorway is going to be under surveillance.'

'If you put a military presence on that road, your mice won't come out to play,' Garrett said.

Elkins shook his head. 'I'm not using soldiers,' he said. 'I've got four E4A surveillance squads out there. They've got all the latest gear, Garrett: hand-held thermal imagers, long-range surveillance viewers, Twiggy night-viewing devices, Davin second-generation weapon sights — '

Garrett held up both hands.

'Sounds good. How many men in each squad?'

'Four,' Elkins said. 'I've got two units disguised as British Telecom repairmen, the first covering the road between the airport and Clady Bridge, the second the stretch between there and the Kilmakee level crossing. I've got two men from the third unit kitted out as surveyors taking theodolite readings at the roundabout on the south side of Templepatrick, two more patrolling the town itself. The fourth unit — two men using an RAC patrol vehicle, two more in an Electricity Board vehicle — will cover the stretch of road from there to the motorway, paying special attention to the bridge over Ballymartin Water, here, and the railway bridge over the motorway feeder road. If Hennessy so much as sticks his nose out, we'll have him.'

'What about DI5 personnel?'

'I'll have a team staking out Aldergrove,' Elkins said. 'If there's going to be a hit, the bandits will have to be at the airport to spot the courier. I want to make sure every one of them is tagged and pictured. I also want to make even more sure nobody switches drivers on my man.'

'Sounds as if you've covered all the angles,' Garrett said. 'How do you cover the stand-in?'

'I'll shadow him all the way in a Q car. He'll be covered from every angle. As well as the E4A teams, we'll also have a helicopter six hundred feet up quartering across the road every five hundred yards. If nothing happens, we'll try again in a few days' time. And keep on doing it until something does happen.'

'All right. Let's assume Hennessy makes a play. What's the response?'

Elkins smiled an almost feline smile. 'Already organized,' he said softly.

'You're going to use the SAS?'

'That's right,' Elkins said. 'I told you, I'm not taking any chances. There's a mole in this place somewhere, and until we find him, I don't want anyone out there I don't trust one hundred per cent.'

'You mean Patterson's people?' Garrett said. 'But if you've called in E4A units, the Chief Constable RUC will have so advised the General Officer Commanding, Northern Ireland. Who in turn will have told MI.'

'No, he won't,' Elkins said, with a self-satisfied smile. 'Because you told him not to.'

'I did what?'

'I told you I'd done my homework, Charles,' Elkins replied smoothly. 'I know how much clout PACT has got. You people can do anything you want to do.'

'Well,' Garrett said. 'If you're making unilateral decisions, I think I'll make one as well.'

'Such as?'

'When that courier pulls out of Aldergrove tomorrow morning, I'm going to be right there in that pursuit car with you.'

Elkins made a wry face. 'You're not really giving me a choice, are you?'

'You know how much clout PACT has got,' Garrett said. 'What do you think?'

★ ★ ★

The security service car was an off-white Vauxhall Cavalier with automatic transmission; as well as a transponder unit, it carried an onboard computer. The boot was packed with miniaturized technology: enough, as Elkins unsmilingly remarked, to track a fish up a river. Its presence today was academic: because it was accepted that the bandits would be monitoring any radio frequency they might use, the security forces would be observing total radio silence.

They watched the courier get into the chauffeured Ford and move out. Elkins moved off in its wake; as he inched the car through the control, Garrett was reminded of taking a vehicle through Checkpoint Charlie in Berlin: chain-link fencing, concrete barriers, antispeed ramps, the eerie sense of being watched by unseen eyes. He leaned back in his seat and watched the courier car eating up the road a quarter of a mile ahead of them. It was almost exactly two miles from the control zone to the bridge under the Antrim road; beyond it at Clady Bridge lay a scattering of white houses, followed by another empty two-mile stretch to the level crossing at Kilmakee. They bumped over the railroad tracks and swung right at the roundabout, through the industrial estate and then the town of Templepatrick itself.

The traffic on the motorway was light; as the courier car ahead went faster, he put his foot down and the needle on the speedometer swung towards the eighty mark. The serried roofs of Newtownabbey stretched off to the north, the wide blue lough and the hills beyond them. Overhead signs indicated a junction approaching: Elkins moved over to the middle lane.

As the triple-striped three-hundred-yard marker flashed by, a dark blue Ford behind them slid into the inside lane and began to accelerate. Garrett glanced at it and saw that the rear window on the driver's side was open. He acted without conscious thought, throwing himself to the right and between the two front seats so that as much of his body as possible was below the level of the door sill. In that same instant, a vicious hail of bullets shattered the windows on Garrett's side, slamming into the bodywork with a noise like a demented jackhammer.

Elkins brought the car to a screaming halt on the emergency shoulder, yelling commands over the transceiver. Garrett raced out of the car, running to the parapet overlooking the exit ramp down which the Ford had raced after the assassination attempt. Up ahead the helicopter was veering back toward their position; police cars slid into position in front of and behind the courier car, which had come to a safe stop a mile ahead.

As Garrett watched, the scene below was played out with murderous speed. Just as the Ford reached the bottom of the exit ramp, an armoured Land Rover roared out in front of it. The driver of the smaller car jammed everything on, skidding from side to side down the narrow ramp, smashing into the side of the Land Rover with a dull, flat, metallic sound like someone slamming a huge refrigerator door.

Two men piled out, machine pistols

blazing. They laid a withering hail of fire down on the 'pig' slewed across the road as they tried to run round it to the roundabout beyond. As Garrett raced down the ramp towards the scene of the collision, the sound of their weapons came up off the steel and stone like fireworks. Then all at once the doors of the Land Rover burst open and men jumped out, firing Browning automatics. Garrett saw the two running men slew to one side as if struck by invisible hands. One of them crumpled into an untidy heap, like a bundle of old clothes left beside the road; the other ran on perhaps another fifteen yards, slowing, slowing, one leg buckling under him. He sat down in the middle of the road and tried to lift the machine pistol. One of the two men who had jumped out of the Land Rover was running toward him. He dropped to one knee and fired three spaced shots. The man sitting in the middle of the road pitched forward and was still.

Garrett stopped; he would prove nothing by running into the killing zone to be shot by some jumpy young SAS man. He looked up as Elkins came hurrying down the ramp, the wind whipping his carefully combed hair into untidy confusion. He held a transceiver in his hand; it was crackling urgently.

'You all right, Garrett?' he shouted. His face was pale, his eyes edgy with the same tension Garrett had noticed earlier.

'They never learn,' Garrett said. 'Not one gun in fifty can put a bullet through the door of a car.' He allowed his mind to dwell only for a moment on what would have happened had the assassin been using Equaloy or one of the other THV — very high speed — loads. They had bullets these days that could punch a hole through a four-inch steel plate.

'I've got a question for you,' he said harshly to Elkins.

'Yes?'

'Why did they attack us and not the courier car?'

Elkins stared at him. 'You think they spotted us at the airport?'

'Somebody told them we'd be on the road. They weren't half as interested in the courier as they were in us. Now I've got another question.'

'Go ahead,' Elkins said.

'Given they went after our car on purpose,' Garrett said, 'which one of us were they trying to kill?'

8

By the time Garrett and Elkins got back to the Stormont complex, the two dead terrorists had been identified. They were Seamus Arnot and Padraic Murphy: two small-time bandits with long police records.

'That was an impressive operation back there,' Garrett complimented Elkins. 'The more so because it was unexpected. What made you think they might try a hit on the motorway?'

'It struck me last night, after you left. You remember when I told you about the E4A teams yesterday, you said the mice wouldn't come out if they were there?'

'I remember. You said they'd be invisible.'

'That was the original plan,' Elkins said. 'But then I thought, if I make sure they can't hit the courier on the Templepatrick road, it will have to be on the motorway. And since there are only two exits between where we joined the road and central Belfast, it seemed a good bet they'd try at one or the other. All I had to do was to tell the E4A squads to make themselves obvious and . . . well, you saw what happened.'

'You make it all sound neat and logical,' Garrett said.

'It was a well-planned operation. Of course, what they didn't know was that we were ready for them. They ran right into my trap.'

'Where were they from, the two in the car?'

'Murphy's originally from Wexford,' Elkins replied. 'Arnot lives — lived — in Craigantlet, a village about halfway between here and Bangor.'

'Any family?'

'It's on Arnot's RUC record,' Elkins said. 'There's a wife, Maureen. No children.'

'That's all we know about him?'

'Until we get the computer dossiers.'

Garrett shrugged. 'May I use your phone?'

Elkins made a help-yourself gesture.

Garrett rang Harry Patterson's office, and as he had expected, Lieutenant Christie answered.

'Major Patterson is at a security co-ordination meeting,' he explained. 'Is there anything I can do for you?'

'I asked Major Patterson for a car, lieutenant,' Garrett said. 'I'd like to know if it's ready. I'd also like to know where I might be sleeping tonight.'

'I've been expecting your call,' Christie said. 'We've got a nice little motor waiting for you down at the car pool. And I've organized a flat: living room, bedroom and bath *en suite*. There's even a small kitchen. It's in Stranmillis Road, right opposite the Botanical Gardens. Really nice area.'

'Well done, lieutenant,' Garrett said. 'I'll be over in a little while.'

'See you then,' Christie said, and hung up. Garrett turned to say goodbye to Elkins and found he was alone in the office. He picked up his coat and went out along the corridor. There was an air of intense activity and bustle that had not been apparent when he first arrived;

obviously DI5 was cock-a-hoop over its victory. It didn't take much to please them, he thought.

The sergeant mechanic who ran over the controls of the Ford that was waiting for him in the car pool told him it was fitted with a Ramjet supercharger.

'At a pinch you can wind her up to a hundred and twenty, sir,' he told Garrett. 'She's screwed down tight so she 'olds the road like a bloody express train. Front and rear bumpers reinforced. Windows fitted with CMC bullet-resistant glass, body panels lined with fibreglass to reduce penetration. She won't stop a Stinger, but nobody will be able to hit you with anything else.'

'At last, the safe car,' Garrett grinned. 'Now tell me, how do I get to Craigantlet?'

'Turn left as you leave the castle,' the sergeant said. 'Go down the road to Dundonald and follow the signs for Bangor. Up over Carrowreagh Hill and you're there. Any problems, you'll find maps in the glove compartment.'

'Right,' Garrett said, and moved off.

He cleared the checkpoint at the gate and drove east on Upper Newtownards Road, past the hospital and on to the little town of Dundonald, turning up the hill when he saw the signposts for Craigantlet and Bangor. The road dropped in a gentle slope to a crossroads; the dozen or so cottages and two-storey houses scattered along the narrow street constituted the village of Craigantlet. The main road ran straight on through woodland about a quarter of a mile ahead. He pulled off the road, locked the car and walked up the street to the pub that stood set back from the main road on a patch of green.

It was called the Dog and Duck, a neat, snug little place with a saloon bar and a lounge with a peat fire glowing in the fireplace. Garrett went into the bar and ordered a half-pint of draught Guinness. The girl who served him was about twenty, a plump and good-natured redhead with a glorious rash of freckles.

'I was wondering if I could ask your help finding someone,' Garrett said to the barmaid. She came across, polishing a glass with a none-too-clean towel. 'Oh, aye?' she said. 'And who would that be?'

'Young fellow by the name of Seamus Arnot,' Garrett said. 'They told me he lives up here.'

'In Craigantlet?' the girl said. She frowned as if she was concentrating, then shook her head. She'd never get an Oscar nomination, Garrett decided. 'Tommy?' she shouted. 'Tommy!'

A burly, balding man in his mid-fifties came through from the other bar. He had the thick body and murky eyes of a one-time sportsman turned drinker.

'Gent here is looking for Seamus Arnot,' the girl said, and went through to the other bar. The man glowered at Garrett with unconcealed hostility.

'You English?'

'That's right,' Garrett replied. 'I'm from London.'

'What's your business with Seamus Arnot?'

'I'm afraid it's confidential,' Garrett said. 'A legal matter. Now, does he live in Craigantlet or not?'

'Go down the street, past the shops. You'll see the little pond with two cottages beside it. The first one is Clonmel Cottage. That's the Arnot place.'

'Good,' Garrett said briskly. 'Can I buy you a drink?'

'Why not,' the man said.

'And I'll have the other half of this,' Garrett told him. He watched as the man drew the beer from the pump and put it overflowing on the terry mat on the counter. He gave him a five-pound note; he took the money but did not drink anything, handing Garrett his change without comment and going back to polishing glasses, his full lower lip stuck out in concentration.

Garrett walked down the street, past a little grocer's and a fruit shop with bunches of cellophane-wrapped dahlias standing in buckets of water outside. Up on the wooded flank of a hill about a quarter of a mile to the north he could see the grey scarred walls of a quarry. The little pond, fenced off to keep dogs out, was choked with green weed that had not deterred the nesting coots and ducks. Beyond it he saw the two single-storey cottages the publican had described. They had whitewashed walls, recessed mullion windows and oak stable-type doors. As he knocked, he did not fail to notice that the front step of Clonmel Cottage was scrubbed and stoned spotlessly clean.

He knocked again; no one stirred. He was about to turn away when the door of the adjoining cottage swung open. He turned to find himself facing a young woman of about thirty wearing a red blouse and a black skirt. She was quite tall, with a willowy figure, fine green eyes and long dark hair.

'Nobody home,' he said, with a gesture at the Arnots' front door.

'Maureen's gone to Bangor,' the woman said. 'Shopping.'

'It was her husband I wanted to see, actually,' he told her.

'Oh?' She said it with just enough enquiry to let him know he could tell her why if he wanted to but she wouldn't take offence if he didn't. He let the question slide past.

'Have you any idea what time Mrs Arnot will be back, Mrs . . . ?'

'Burke,' the woman said. 'Patricia Burke. There's a bus from Bangor that gets here about a quarter past. I expect she'll be on that.'

'My name is Charles Garrett,' he told her. 'I'm from London. A business matter I have to see Mr Arnot about.'

She looked at her wrist watch. 'It's only half a hour,' she said. 'You could wait here if you like. Come in, I'll make you a cup of tea.'

He went into the cottage, stepping straight off the street into a neat living room. On the end wall was a recessed fireplace cluttered with highly polished brassware, flanked on each side by cluttered bookshelves, one of which held a mini hi-fi stack. Against the wall facing him was a two-seater sofa with a glass-topped coffee table beside it. In one corner was a small portable TV; above it he could see through a hatch into what was obviously an equally neat and compact kitchen. Beside the stripped pine Welsh dresser on the wall near the street door was another door: the bedroom or bedrooms, he guessed.

'Pretty room,' he said. 'Are the beams original?'

'I believe so,' Patricia Burke said, going into the kitchen. 'How do you like your tea — with milk or lemon?'

'Milk is fine,' he said, leaning on the door jamb. The kitchen was bright and cheerful, with a larger window looking out on to a vegetable garden and a postage-stampsized patch of lawn. 'How long have you lived here, Mrs Burke?'

'Eight years,' she said. 'And to save you asking, I'm a widow.'

Garrett smiled. 'I *was* wondering,' he said. 'It's a very feminine house.'

'Is that a compliment?'

'It was meant to be,' he said. He watched as she put the teapot on to the spout of the kettle and left it there so that when the water boiled the steam warmed the pot. She put two measures of tea in the pot and filled it with hot water, then put a tea cosy over it. Taking two cups and saucers out of a cupboard next to the cooker, and two teaspoons out of a drawer beneath the sink unit, she put them on a tray. She opened a circular tin

138

box and put some biscuits on a plate. Then she placed a milk jug and sugar basin next to them on the tray, and he held the door open as she went into the living room and put the tray on the table by the windows looking out into the street.

'No sugar,' he said, as she poured. She nodded and handed him a cup.

'You say you're from England, Mr Garrett?' she said. It was put in the form of a question but it wasn't one that required an answer.

'London.' he said.

'I didn't know the Arnots had friends in London.'

'We're not friends,' he said. 'As I said, I'm over here on business. I met Seamus in Belfast. He told me he had some . . . goods for sale.'

Her expression altered. She stood up, putting her cup down firmly on the table.

'I think I'd like you to leave my house,' she said 'Immediately, please.'

Garrett stood up. 'Of course,' he said. 'Do you mind telling me why?'

'I don't wish to discuss it,' she said.

'Just keep your dirty business to yourself!'

'Mrs Burke, please — '

'Would you prefer I call the police?'

'That won't be necessary,' Garrett said. 'But let me ask you just one question before I go. What do you think I came up here for?'

'I don't know, and I don't want to know.'

'What does he sell, Mrs Burke? Guns, is it? Or something else?'

She shook her head, holding the door open.

'Let me just say one more thing. I came here to question Maureen Arnot about her husband.'

She frowned. 'I don't understand.'

'He's a member of the IRA, isn't he?'

Her face stiffened. She shook her head vehemently. 'Who are you?'

'Seamus Arnot was killed while trying to assassinate two security service officers yesterday,' he told her. Her eyes widened with shock; she reached behind her until she could touch the back of the chair, then sat down slowly, staring up at him.

'There was nothing on the news,' she

whispered. 'In the papers . . . '

'No,' he said. 'We haven't released the information yet.'

'Then you — you're — '

'That's right.'

'Oh, poor Maureen,' she said softly. 'Oh, the poor thing.'

'You don't think she knew her husband was a terrorist?'

Patricia Burke looked at him as if she was seeing him for the first time. 'How easily you people use that word,' she said. There was more regret than contempt in her voice.

'You sound as if you've had personal experience.'

'Oh, yes,' she said. 'Oh, yes.'

'Your husband?'

'Antony James Michael Burke,' she said, a faraway look in her eyes. 'I used to call him Ant. We lived in Derry then. I knew he was part of it, there was no way he could keep something like that from me. The East Tyrone Brigade, they called it. As if it was part of an army.'

'That's the way they see themselves, Mrs Burke.'

'I know, I know.' She said it with a sigh. 'He thought he was a hero, fighting for a United Ireland. He was just . . . expendable.'

'How was he killed?'

'He was with a man called McCaffery. They — '

'Patrick McCaffery?'

She turned to face him, eyebrows raised. 'You've heard of him?'

'Mad Pat, they called him,' Garrett said. 'Yes, I've heard of him.'

'A man came to see me later. He never told me his name. He just said the Brits had killed Ant. At a place called Portnoo in County Donegal. Something to do with a shipment of guns.'

As she told him the rest of the story, Garrett sat silent, stunned by the enormity of the coincidence. Antony Burke had been one of four men who died in a gunfight at Portnoo when Paddy McCaffery's unit, there to pick up an illicit shipment of guns coming in off a freighter, had been ambushed by an Army unit. And it had been Charles Garrett, operating out of Security Services Liaison at Lisburn — the Rathole — who had masterminded the operation.

'I swore as God was my witness that I would set my face against the men of violence from that day forward,' Patricia Burke was saying, her voice intense, her eyes empty of expression. 'And I have done so ever since. That was why when you said you'd come to buy something off Seamus Arnot, I thought you must be one of them.'

'Have you got any idea what he was handling, Mrs Burke?'

She shook her head vehemently. 'I didn't want to know. I'd see them coming to the house. You could always tell, they'd knock on the door, he'd come out, and they'd all go up the road to the Dog and Duck. Then next day, or a few days later, there'd be another bombing.'

Semtex, he thought. Arnot was an armourer, handling plastic explosives. 'Can you recall any specific instances?'

She shook her head. 'I made a point of not remembering, Mr Garrett. I know these people. They're animals. You know what they do to informers?'

'I know,' Garrett said. The savagery of the IRA punishment squads had made the Royal Victoria Hospital in Belfast a world leader in orthopedic surgery. Nobody knew for sure how many men had been dragged out of their homes or cars or pubs by hooded men to be 'knee-capped' — shot through both knees and, sometimes, the ankles and elbows as well.

'What about his wife? You think she knew?'

'The women always know, Mr Garrett,' she said. 'Some of them glory in it, some of them hate it. You'll not get one of them to talk about it.'

'Maybe not,' he said. 'But we've got to try, just the same. Do you know anything about the Arnots?'

'Only what she tells me.

'Was there any man or group of men who visited the house regularly?'

'There was one,' she said thoughtfully. 'I don't know his name. He's about forty. Red hair and very blue eyes — startling blue, if you know what I mean.'

'I know exactly what you mean,'

Garrett said. *Hennessy? Was it possible?* 'Anything you can tell me about him?'

'He has a very bad limp,' Patricia Burke said. 'As if one leg is shorter than the other.'

'Left leg or right?'

She frowned, trying to remember. 'Left, I think. Yes, left.'

In the eye of his memory, Garrett saw Sean Hennessy poised on the rail of the bridge over the Elbe in Lauenburg, heard again his defiant shout as he leaped off. In that same instant Garrett had fired a tight group of three shots at the moving figure. *They said he was shot up*, Danny had told him. *Damned near died.* Hennessy had not escaped scot-free.

'Did this man stay with the Arnots?'

She shook her head. 'They usually went off in a car. Sometimes he'd be gone for two or three days.'

'Do you know where they went together?'

'I asked Maureen once. She said they'd gone to the country club.'

'Country club?' It was so unlikely that he laughed.

145

'That was my reaction, too,' Patricia Burke said, smiling for the first time. Her austere expression changed to one of great warmth; he realized that she was a beautiful woman. 'But that was what Maureen used to say: 'Seamus is at the country club.''

'Did she ever tell you the name of this place?'

'I asked her that, too, making it sound, you know, as if I didn't believe a word she was saying. 'Sure and of course I know,' she said. 'Up on the hills above Donaghadee.''

'Well, well,' Garrett said. 'I'm glad I met you, Mrs Burke.'

She nodded absently, watching the street outside through her pretty ruched curtains. 'Tell me,' she asked, 'did you come here alone?'

'Yes, why?'

'Then that man across the street isn't with you?'

Garrett looked out of the window. He was about twenty-three or four, slim, dark-haired. He wore a tan anorak, jeans and trainers.

'What's at the back?' Garrett asked Patricia Burke, his voice urgent.

'The garden,' she said, her breathing quickening. 'A footpath. It goes up the hill to the quarry and Cairn Wood.'

'Go into the kitchen,' Garrett told her. 'Look outside. Tell me if there's anyone out there.'

She nodded and went into the other room. He heard her feet moving sibilantly on the tiled floor. She came back in.

'I can't see anyone,' she whispered.

He went into the kitchen and looked out into the tiny garden. A four-foot-high fence divided it from the Arnots' garden next door. The ground sloped slightly uphill; at the end of the garden were two dwarf apple trees and beyond them a copse of what looked like black cherry trees.

'Is there someone there?' she asked. Her face was pale and set.

He shrugged. 'More than likely. They hunt in packs.'

'Wait,' she said. She went across to the sofa and picked up a shawl, throwing it around her shoulders. Before he could stop her she had opened the door and gone out into the street, crossing to where the young man in the anorak was standing.

'What are you doing here?' she said to him.

'What?' he barked, as if unable to believe his ears.

'I asked you what you are doing here. Who are you waiting for?'

'Bog off, woman!' he snapped, pushing off the wall with his foot.

'Don't use that kind of language with me!' she snapped back. 'We don't want your sort around here. If you don't move along, I will call the police.'

'A'm not a fuckin' burglar, woman, A'm waitin' for a friend!' the man told her angrily. 'Get on about your business, now.'

While the man's attention was firmly fixed on Patricia Burke, Garrett slid out of the back door of the cottage. He vaulted cleanly over the low fence and started up the footpath at an easy lope. As he did, he saw a man step out into the path about twenty feet in front of him, lifting a pistol that looked as big as a field gun. He reacted instantaneously, throwing himself to one side into the bushes bordering the path and whipping the ASP conversion Smith & Wesson out of his shoulder holster as the crouching man ahead of him opened fire.

The flat bark of the pistol merged with the sharper stutter of the automatic. Bullets plopped into the soft earth alongside Garrett's rolling body as his own shots hit the gunman in an ascending line as neat as coat buttons stitched from windpipe to sternum. The gunman's legs unhinged and he fell forward without a sound.

When he heard the shots, the eyes of the man Patricia Burke had distracted blazed with anger. 'Ye're dead, ye fuckin' bitch!' he shouted, thrusting her aside. He ran across the road past the side of the cottage and stopped in the centre of the footpath a few yards from where his partner lay sprawled. He moved forward a few feet at a time, his body crouched in the classic firing stance, a Browning automatic clutched in both hands sweeping the area before him in a repeating semicircle. Garrett stepped soundlessly out of the shrubs behind him.

'Boo,' he said.

The man in the anorak whirled about on his toes and screamed something unintelligible as he pulled the trigger, but his aim was nothing like careful enough. As his bullets smacked chunks of plaster off the wall of Patricia Burke's cottage, Garrett carefully and deliberately shot him, first through both arms and then one leg. The terrorist folded to the floor, screeching with pain and frustration as Garrett ran across and kicked the weapon away from his clawing, bloody fingers.

'You fuckin' bastard,' the man raged, kicking out at him ineffectually with his good leg. 'Fuckin' bastard, you've fuckin' crippled me!'

Garrett nodded. 'I know,' he said. 'No fun, is it?'

9

The big white house stood on rising ground about half a mile north of the little fishing town of Donaghadee. Below it, terraced gardens sloped down to the gate on the coast road; beyond the road, the cliffs fell steeply to the rocky shore. Over the blue water, perhaps a mile offshore, was the rocky hump of Copeland Island. Although it was quite a conventional building, Craigthomas House was unusual in the sense that there were few such grand manors any more in Northern Ireland: an imposing mansion approached by a curving drive that led between mature beech trees to a turning circle in front of the graceful Georgian façade.

It had come on the market only twice since 1905. On this second occasion, Craigthomas was immediately purchased by the IRA — through nominees using one of its many Swiss bank accounts — as a safe house where top-level strategy conferences could be held. A number of improvements were made without benefit of planning permission while Craigthomas was converted into a convalescent home for wealthy private patients — a cover, and a profitable one, for its other, unadvertised use.

With this cover established, the IRA was then able, when it so wished, to arrange for its own people to be looked after at Craigthomas at the expense of the genuine patients. Battle-weary street fighters, men who had suffered at the hands of the heavies at Castlereagh interrogation centre, or whose health had broken in the Kesh, front-liners who had taken a bullet and could not be treated by any legitimate doctor or hospital, were sent to the 'country club', for de-stressing. A stay at Craigthomas was perceived as an honour not unlike being awarded a decoration.

It had been at Craigthomas, in the long conference room with its green baize-covered tables and oil paintings of long-forgotten race-horses, that Sean

Hennessy had proposed the plan which was now in operation. It was to the same venue that he and the members of his unit had now been summoned to appear before a strategy review board of the Army Council.

He came ready for a fight. It was like some sort of fucking sales conference for chocolate bars or paperback books, he decided as he surveyed the group of men at the top table, with little nameplates in front of each executive to show how important he was. Pudgy Thomas Shannon, chairman of the five-man board; William Black, executive officer; John Ferguson, Sean McNamee and James Birch, advisers.

Advisers! Shopkeepers and bloody insurance salesmen, he thought, glaring at the men who had been chosen to review his actions; when was the last time any of you heard a fucking shot fired in anger? The wound in his hip throbbed as if in sympathy. Review boards! Committees! As if you would ever get rid of the fucking British by *discussing* it!

'All right, gentlemen,' Shannon said.

He looked like what he was, the owner of a butcher's shop in Ballyhackamore. 'Let's begin. You all have an agenda. The first item is the matter of the courier assassinations. For those members of the board who are not familiar with the background, I'll call on Sean Hennessy to outline the thinking behind them. Sean?'

He sat back in his chair and regarded Hennessy with an expressionless stare. Hennessy took his time about replying, feeling the weight of the regard of his own men. They were as good a team as could be got these days. It was harder and harder to get men as experienced as those he had lost in Germany. He had picked carefully: Michael Conlan, his second in command; his two non-coms, Peter Nash and a thickset tough from the Bogside called Jimmy Bounden; the five 'soldiers', Bob Povah, Alan Riddoch, Georgie Steele, Ronnie Williams and John Penketh. Good men, all of them. Fire in their bellies, not like this bloodless lot sent to pass judgement on their actions.

He stood up. He knew, of course, that Shannon and his kind viewed him and his unit as wild dogs that had to be muzzled and kept on a tight choke chain. Fuck them all. If they were expecting him to grovel because one or two things had gone wrong, they'd die of old age waiting. Show one sign of weakness and the bastards would be at your throat like wolves.

'Chairman, gentlemen. Before I begin, I'd like to brief the members of this board on the background of the man who is the target of our operation. His name is Charles Garrett. Does any one of you know anything about him?'

They were silent, as he had known they would be. He almost smiled; too busy promoting their own interests to know or care what the British security forces were really up to. If these were the kind of men in charge of its destiny, he was more than ever glad he had insisted that his unit would be operating independently of the army. He glanced around the table, meeting the eyes of his own men. Watch me, lads, he told them silently, I'll show the bastards.

'I'll take the liberty of assuming your

silence indicates the answer is negative, gentlemen,' he said, making sure there was not so much as a hint of sarcasm in his tone. 'And tell you exactly who Charles Garrett is. Now, a while ago I mentioned Paddy McCaffery. You'll all remember him, of course?'

There was a murmur of agreement: in the circles these men moved in, there were certain names one never forgot. Patrick McCaffery's was one of them, and even someone who would not have known Mad Pat if he'd walked into the room accompanied by Jesus Christ and a band of archangels would have been very loth to admit otherwise.

'I'll take you back a few years,' Hennessy said. 'There'll be those here who might not know just what Paddy did for this organization.'

McCaffery, he reminded them, had been the IRA's first organizational genius. A tall, skinny fellow with a shock of black hair and Kerry green eyes, he had become a fighting member of the army in 1960, on his eighteenth birthday. By the time he was twenty, he was a veteran, by twenty-five an officer, and a year later a maximum-security prisoner in the British Army prison at Long Kesh. The story of his escape from there was now a legend to rank with the springing of George Blake: one visiting day, his brother Peter, a priest, smuggled a clerical suit into the Kesh, and the two of them walked out under the noses of the security forces, giving a blessing to the arseholes guarding the gates as they left.

From that day forward, Paddy was on the run, working out of safe houses just across the border in Cavan and Monaghan. The more he ran the gauntlet, the more he perceived that until they created an intelligence service as good, if not better than the one they were up against, they were risking a hiding every time they put up an operation. To do that, they needed finance, big money. Mad Pat put his days of violence behind him, devoting all his time and not inconsiderable energy to finding ways and means of getting it.

He began by persuading the council to stop thinking like Chicago gangsters. He outlawed the bank robberies and thick-ear protection rackets that had flourished throughout Northern Ireland. He persuaded the council to found and finance bona fide security firms which netted exactly the same levies as before, but openly and legitimately. Next, he organized the takeover of the taxi trade, so that nothing and no one moved on the streets of Belfast and Derry that the army did not know about. At the same time, McCaffery established links with Middle Eastern governments sympathetic to the aims of the IRA and opened the Swiss bank accounts that made it possible to wash the finances now flowing in, from these new allies, from NORAID in North America and from the business enterprises he had set up.

When that was done, he channelled these Persil-white funds into legitimate building and construction firms, in turn directing the profits from these into the purchase of arms and ammunition with which to continue the struggle. He opened up worldwide networks for arms supplies: in the United States, in South

America, in Bulgaria and the Far East. And in the process, he became the Most Sought and Most Wanted fugitive in Ireland. British Security tried every trick in its not inconsiderable book to try and capture Mad Paddy, but they never had any luck until Charles Garrett came along.

'Now I'll tell you about this man Garrett,' Hennessy said. 'He's something of a special case. He came out here as a member of a new unit they called the Ratcatchers. They operated out of Security Liaison Headquarters in Lisburn — that's how it became known as the Rathole. They were all new, and our people knew none of them. That was how they got their first breakthrough.'

The British set up a plan so carefully constructed and convincingly mounted that nobody even suspected it was a trap. Even so, every precaution that could be taken was taken, everyone involved checked and double checked. It all looked clean and green. An IRA scout in New York had a contact who promised them a quarter-of-a-million-pound package of

Redeye missiles, grenade launchers and Heckler & Koch sub-machine-guns through a supplier in Italy. The scout in New York, Brian McGuinness, got the green light: make the buy. Everything went as merry as a marriage bell until the trawler bringing the shipment into Portnoo, a little fishing village on the south coast of Gweebarra Bay in Donegal, was on its way into harbour.

'We got a call from New York. One of our people had recognized the middle-man we were dealing with as a British military intelligence officer he'd known in Germany. He was calling himself Liam Brady, but his real name was Charles Garrett. We knew we'd been had, but it was too late. Paddy McCaffery and his boys were already at the rendezvous, waiting to make the pick-up.'

The Army was lying in wait for McCaffery and his team; three British soldiers and four of Mad Pat's men were killed in the fight that followed. McCaffery and the other five were arrested. It was a major setback; apart from the loss of funds and the death of good soldiers,

McCaffery was a bearer of secrets. The Brits would take him apart like a child deconstructing a Lego building, piece by piece, brick by brick. Getting him out of their clutches before that happened became a matter of the utmost priority.

'Hard on the heels of them taking Paddy, we had a bit of luck,' Hennessy went on. 'We found out that Garrett — he was using the name Antrim at the time — was living in a nice big house in Lisburn. We put watchers on the house; there was just Garrett and his wife Diana living there. Two days later we lifted the wife on the road from Glenavy to Lisburn and put her into isolation.'

How long are you going to keep me here?

As long as necessary.

What's your name?

You can call me Sean.

Why are you looking at me like that?

I don't know. You're shivering.

I'm afraid. I'm afraid all the time.

Don't be afraid. I won't hurt you.

Don't touch me. Don't put your dirty hands on me.

You want me to. You want it.

No. No.

You do. Say it.

Yes. Yes.

'What happened then?' someone asked, and Hennessy realized his voice had trailed off as he relived his memories.

'We told the Brits we'd make a straight trade, the wife for Paddy McCaffery. No tricks, no surprises, or we'd kill her on the spot. They agreed. I set up the meet, picked the safest place I could find, a crossroads near Fintona. Garrett was to bring Pat and I'd bring the woman.

Will I ever see you again?

No. Never.

'In spite of everything, they double-crossed us,' he concluded. 'They used Garrett, shot Paddy in the head and tried to kill me. The woman was killed as well. I tried to get Garrett but it was no use, I knew the helicopters would already be off the ground. I ran for it.'

'Would it be too much to hope,' a voice interposed, 'that there is a point to this somewhat lengthy monologue?' The speaker was a small, alert-looking man wearing a charcoal-grey suit with a yellow waistcoat beneath it. His name was John Ferguson. He looked like a retired jockey. He had angular features and sharp, intelligent eyes. Michael Conlan caught Hennessy's eye and nodded. Hennessy knew what the signal meant: watch out for this one.

'Aye, there's a point, Mr Ferguson,' he said, heavily. 'From that day on, Charles Garrett was at the top of our Most Wanted list. But he just disappeared off the face of the earth. We put our best people on the job of finding him, but nobody could. Then he reappeared last autumn. In Germany.'

'Ah, yes.' It was the soft-voiced Ferguson again. 'Your Remembrance Sunday operation in Lauenburg. Garrett trashed that, too, didn't he?'

'He trashed nothing!' Hennessy replied hotly. 'We were compromised by a damned fool who sent picture postcards to some German girl he'd been shacking up with on the sly. Garrett's part in the whole thing was incidental.'

'I've heard it told differently,' Ferguson

insisted. 'Are you going to tell us it wasn't Garrett who shot Tony Gallagher at Lauenburg and put a bullet in your hip that nearly killed you, too?'

He felt as if he had been stabbed with a red-hot iron. Sickness roared through him. He teetered on the parapet of the bridge and then went over, down and down to the dark purling water. It was like hitting liquid ice, a smashing shock that tore a scream of pain which came out of his throat as a bubbling growl no one else could hear in the turning green darkness.

Every fibre of his being screamed at him to go up, but he made himself stay beneath the water, letting the fast-moving river carry him beneath the bridge and out of range of the guns above.

Then when he tried to swim, the pain.

Death was there, grinning at him.

Let me live, you old bastard, he begged.

Let me live till I kill Garrett.

'We've been trying to find Garrett for years,' Hennessy said angrily. 'He's been under sentence of death since Paddy

McCaffery was killed. Until I saw him at Lauenburg, we didn't know where to look for him. After that, it was easier. As some of you will know, we have our own sources inside British security. We put them on to the job of locating Garrett.'

'And?' The speaker this time was Thomas Shannon. He gave Ferguson a sideways scowl as he spoke. It was clear he didn't like the way the younger man was dominating the questioning.

'They ran into all sorts of closed doors,' Hennessy said. 'All we could learn was that Garrett was part of something new, a counterterrorist unit so secret no mention of it has ever appeared in print. The Brits simply don't admit it exists. But it's there. And anything this organization decides to do takes precedence over any parallel action being taken by Army intelligence, DI5 or DI6 or anyone else.'

'This is all very interesting, chairman,' John Ferguson said urbanely. 'But what's it to do with assassinating DI5 couriers?'

'Have you ever heard of something called the 'response syndrome', Mr Ferguson?' Hennessy asked, leading him into it. Ferguson frowned and shook his head.

'Well, I don't imagine they use the term much in farming,' Hennessy said, putting in the knife of his contempt and twisting it. 'I'll explain it to you.'

It was a well-tried terrorist formula, he explained, to threaten or even actually carry out a killing or a bombing, and then to minutely monitor every aspect of the security response to it. Once you knew how the enemy would react — and he had no choice but to do so — it was child's play to outwit him next time such an attack took place.

'Our first action was to form a new unit to bring Garrett out into the open, with myself as commander since I'm the only one knows him by sight. We knew that bombings and sectarian killings were ignored. So it had to be something . . . more spectacular. That was why the courier assassinations were mounted. We wanted to see what kind of attack would bring Garrett's organization into action.'

'And if that hadn't worked . . . ?' someone asked.

'It worked,' Hennessy said. 'London reacted just the way we thought they would. Our source inside Stormont reported that Garrett had arrived and we made immediate plans to execute him.'

'Was this the ambush at Newtownabbey?' Ferguson asked, in that irritating way he had. Hennessy scowled at him.

'I'm going to intercede on Sean's behalf here,' Thomas Shannon said, placing his hand flat on the table. 'There are matters of security involved which preclude our discussing the Newtownabbey ambush further. Suffice it to say we mourn the loss of our two brave comrades Padraic Murphy and Seamus Arnot. We'll move on to the events of last Tuesday at Craigantlet.'

He sat back in his chair and regarded Ferguson with an expressionless stare. Hennessy stifled a smile; Shannon was putting Ferguson in his place by reminding him that he was not a bearer of secrets and therefore not privy to discussions involving top-security matters. One for our side, he thought, and turned to face his own men.

'I'll call on Peter Nash, who was in charge of the Craigantlet operation,' he said. Nash stood up. He was a thinfaced man of about forty who held the rank of sergeant in the army. He looked at Hennessy reproachfully. Hennessy met his look with cold disdain. Nash knew the rules just like anybody else: do it right and the sun shone out of your backside. Fuck up and you carried the can on your own: failure had no friends.

'Where do you want me to start?' he said to Shannon.

'At the beginning, Peter,' Shannon said, smiling benignly. 'Start at the beginning.'

'Right,' Nash said, rubbing his bony hands together as if to get them warm. 'It was Tuesday, after lunch. We got a call from Tommy Padstow, the landlord of the Dog and Duck at Craigantlet. He said there was a fellow asking about Seamus Arnot. English by the sound of him, he said, and a pig by the look of him. Now, as yez all know, Seamus had been killed by the SAS at Newtownabbey only two days earlier, so as soon as I got the call I whistled up two of the lads and we went up to Craigantlet.'

'You knew your men had gone up there, Sean?'

Hennessy shook his head. 'I was . . . elsewhere. Meeting someone.'

'What time of day was this, Peter?' someone asked.

'Teatime,' Nash replied. 'People were coming home from work.'

'Go on.'

'When we got to Craigantlet, I went to the pub to talk to Tommy Padstow; he told us the Englishman had gone down the street to see Seamus' wife. I sent Dermot Flaherty and Charlie Sillery to check. My idea was to lift him, get him into the car and away where we could question him and find out what he was up to. So while Dermot and Charlie went down the street, I went back to the car. I wanted to be ready to get out fast.'

'Any comments on that?' Shannon asked, looking at the others around the table.

'What did you do when you got to the car?' The speaker was Sean McNamee, sitting on Shannon's right, a saturnine, balding man whose dark sweater with a white polo neck beneath it gave him the appearance of a priest.

'I waited where I'd parked it,' Nash said, raising his eyebrows as if the question surprised him. 'By the pub.'

'I see,' McNamee said gravely, nodding to the others as if Nash's words were especially significant. 'You don't think it might have been better if you'd gone down there yourself, left one of the others in charge of the motor? Surely it's a squad commander's job to be at the sharp end?'

Shannon looked up. 'What do you have to say to that, Peter?'

'We didn't know anything about this fellow who was asking questions,' Nash replied, twin spots of colour on his cheeks betraying his indignation. 'Whether he was alone or part of a team. I sent the boys down to suss him out. I didn't know it was going to turn into the fucking gunfight at the fucking OK corral.'

'No one is criticizing you,' Shannon said, holding up his hands. 'This isn't a

170

disciplinary meeting, we're just trying to get the facts. Go on, please.'

'Not much more to tell,' Nash replied, not completely mollified. 'When they got down the street the boys found the Englishman was talking to a woman named Burke who lives next door to the Arnots.'

'Patricia Burke,' Hennessy interposed. 'I checked on her. She's a schoolteacher. No affiliations, but seeing she's the widow of Tony Burke, we've nothing to worry about. Burke was one of the lads who were killed by the Brits when Paddy McCaffery was taken at Portnoo in '77, so his widow will have no reason to love them.'

'Sure, I didn't know that, did I?' Nash said, irritated. 'And neither did the boys. The plan was simple. Dermot was to go around the back of the house, while Charlie Sillery kept watch from across the road. They were to wait till the Englishman came out, then close in. I'd wheel the car up, and we'd lift him.'

'What went wrong?'

'I don't know. My guess is he spotted

Charlie and sent the woman out to distract him. While she was talking, the Englishman did a bunk out of the back door. I didn't see what happened next, but I heard shots, and I saw Charlie running across the road with his gun in his hand. I knew something had gone wrong. As far as I was able to make out, Dermot was waiting for the Englishman behind the house, but the Englishman just blew him away. Charlie must have run straight into trouble. By the time I got down the street, it was all over. I could see two bodies on the ground, and a crowd gathering. There was nothing I could do. I knew the police would be there any minute, so I got out.'

'Flaherty and Sillery are dead, then?' Shannon asked.

Nash looked at Hennessy. 'Flaherty's dead,' Hennessy announced. 'Charlie Sillery was wounded in both arms and one leg; he's in the maximum-security wing of the Army hospital at Stormont.'

Meaningful looks were exchanged among the members of the committee sitting around the table; if the Brits had Charlie Sillery, it was only going to be a matter of time before they started sweating what he knew out of him.

'How much does Sillery know about your unit?' Ferguson asked. 'Can he endanger your operation?'

Hennessy shook his head. 'We've nothing to fear there,' he said reassuringly. 'Sillery only knew what he needed to know. I assume that to be the very minimum.'

'I'm relieved to hear it,' Ferguson persisted quietly. 'Your record is less than impressive so far, Sean. We've lost four good men on the street, five if we count Charlie Tarr. I think we have the right to wonder whether this operation has not been compromised past all credibility.'

'Point taken.' Shannon gave Ferguson a look. He didn't like the way the younger man was taking control of the meeting again. 'John suggests you're dangerously compromised, Sean. What's your thinking on that?'

'My thinking on that is that John Ferguson is full of what makes the grass grow green,' Hennessy said bitingly, enjoying the startled expressions his words brought to the faces of those around the table. He gave his own boys a look: did this whey-faced bunch of nobodies think they could throw him?

'Now see here, Sean — ' Shannon began, but Hennessy cut him off without mercy.

'No, you listen to me, all of you, and listen carefully,' he snapped. 'My unit was created to take Charles Garrett off the map, and we are going to do it. We have had to make certain . . . accommodations to protect a source who is close enough to Garrett to put him up for us the way a dog puts up a rabbit.'

'Are you telling us you have a spy inside security headquarters?' Ferguson said incredulously.

'I'm telling you we have a way of taking Garrett out of the picture,' Hennessy said. 'All we need is a shooter, the best we have.'

'You want to hire a professional?' Shannon muttered. 'They don't come cheap, Sean.'

'Neither do informants inside Stormont Castle,' Hennessy said. 'Group action is out of the question: we can't take the chance of endangering our source. The only way to be certain of success is to give the job to someone who can do it on a one-to-one basis. And there's only one name in the hat when it comes to that kind of work.'

They stared at him without speaking; he had them. They knew it and he knew it. They would endorse his recommendation because they couldn't come up with a better one, and the executive committee would approve it for the same reason, especially when they learned the identity of the designated assassin. Get on with it, you dozy bugger, he thought impatiently, staring at Thomas Shannon. Shannon looked helplessly at the other members of his review board. Even Ferguson avoided his eyes. Hennessy smiled grimly. They had come to Donaghadee expecting to make him toe their line; instead they were toeing his. Thomas Shannon drew in a deep breath and let it out again.

'Do you have in mind who I think you have in mind?' he asked Hennessy.

'Of course,' Hennessy said laconically. 'May Nolan. The Banshee.'

10

Patterson leaned back in his chair and drew in a deep breath. 'Whose side are you on, Garrett?' he asked.

'Do I have to be on someone's side?'

'You know what I'm talking about. There's a war on here. Elkins wants control of the whole caboodle. The only way he can get it is to put my balls in the wringer. I wouldn't like to think you're helping him.'

'I'm not.'

'Then why the hell didn't you tell me Elkins had an operation on?'

'Elkins told me he doesn't trust your people,' Garrett said, giving it to him straight. 'He thinks there's a top-level security leak, and he thinks it comes from your department.'

'Jesus,' Patterson said, visibly controlling his temper. 'What a bastard. Let me ask you a question, Garrett. Why did the IRA attack your car and not the one with the courier in it?'

'Either they wanted to kill Elkins or they wanted to kill me.'

'You think they were trying to kill Elkins?'

'It's possible.'

'Why would they want to kill him?'

'That's a stupid question.'

'No, I'm serious. If you're suggesting it was because he's DI6, they could hit him any time.

'That means you think I was the target.'

'Nah,' Patterson said. The dark glasses concealed any expression that might have been in the shaded eyes behind them. Which, of course, was why Patterson wore them, Garrett thought.

'All right,' he said. 'I'm listening.'

'Look what happened, Garrett,' Patterson said, leaning forward. 'Two deadbeats take a crack at you. They try to hit you on the motorway; they don't even have armour-piercing ammunition — the whole thing is Mickey Mouse stuff. I say it was a bullshit operation. Window dressing. They just forget to tell the men who were pulling it that the whole thing is being done to make it look as if Elkins is at risk. Then before you or I or anyone else can collar them there's an SAS team, put there by Elkins, waiting to waste them.'

'I can't see it.'

'There's been no announcement about the death of the two men, has there? No radio eulogy, no communiqué saying they died in action, none of the usual bullshit?'

'Not that I know of.'

'Doesn't that make you think?'

'Lots of things make me think, major,' Garrett said evenly. 'Like this game the two of you are playing. You say Elkins is bent, he says you are. And we all go round in circles. Everything you just said about Elkins could as easily apply to you.'

'Not everything,' Patterson said. 'Who knew you were going to Craigantlet?'

Garrett hesitated, and Patterson's thin lips parted in a smile. 'Elkins, right?'

'I asked him about Seamus Arnot. Where he lived.'

Patterson spread his hands: *there, you see?* 'He wasn't with you at Craigantlet. So they could take a crack at you without endangering him.'

Garrett shook his head. 'Not so fast, major,' he said. 'Elkins couldn't possibly have known what I had in mind.'

'He didn't need to,' Patterson said tiredly. 'All he had to do was wait. He's got you under surveillance.'

Garrett frowned. 'There's only one way you could know that.'

Patterson grinned, a wolfish, unrepentant smile. 'Somebody's got to keep an eye on you.'

Garrett shook his head. 'You people,' he said impatiently. 'Why didn't you just stick a neon sign on me?'

'Did you see my operatives?'

'No,' Garrett said. 'But I wasn't looking for them.'

'You wouldn't have seen them if you were,' Patterson said.

'Look, major, I can't work dragging a tail half a mile long around with me,' Garrett said. 'Call off your dogs.'

Patterson nodded. 'You'll be on your own out there,' he said. 'Are you sure that's what you want?'

'Just pass the word,' Garrett said,

getting up. 'If I see anyone on my tail after tonight, I'll assume it's enemy action and act accordingly.'

'You're a blockhead,' Patterson said, without heat. 'But if that's what you want, all right, you're a Manx cat: no tail. Where are you going now?'

'To see Elkins and tell him what I just told you,' Garrett said. 'Then I've got a date with an old friend.'

Patterson raised his eyebrows. 'Anyone I know?'

Garrett shook his head. 'Before your time, major,' he said. 'Long before your time.'

★　★　★

A couple of hours later Garrett strolled over to Donegall Square East, stopping once or twice to look in shop windows. He got on a bus for Balmoral, taking a seat inside near the platform and ignoring the other passengers. He waited until the driver started to pull away from the stop, then swung off. He walked rapidly across to a number 69 bus that was just leaving, and jumped aboard for the short journey south through the city to the Botanic Gardens. He smiled; just because Elkins and Patterson had promised to take off the tail didn't mean they had actually done so. If there had been anyone following him, the man was probably halfway to Balmoral by now.

He got off the bus at the Botanic Gardens. It wasn't difficult to find the high-domed Palm House; it looked a bit like a glass version of the Dome of the Rock in Jerusalem, rearing high above the trees at the centre of the manicured grounds. Garrett ambled along the pathway, a copy of the *Independent* tucked beneath his arm. An old lady was sitting on the bench in front of the tree with a plaque which identified it as *Sassafras albidum*.

'Good afternoon,' Garrett said. 'Would you mind if I sat here?'

The woman glared at him. 'Not at all,' she said.

She rolled shut the brown paper bag of breadcrumbs from which she had been feeding the birds and put it into a plastic

181

shopping bag. She got up and fastened her coat, an old grey woollen number with a moth-eaten fur collar.

Garrett waited until she was gone, using the newspaper to conceal his careful check of the surrounding area. There were very few people about; a couple sitting on a bench a few hundred yards away, an elderly man walking with a golden retriever.

'She was only the mortician's daughter,' a familiar voice intoned. Garrett looked around to see Danny Flynn grinning at him.

'Hello, Danny.'

'You're supposed to say, 'but anybody cadaver',' Flynn said, petulantly.

'You're spending a lot of money.'

'What you want to know doesn't come cheap, Mr Garrett. These people you're interested in, they're mad dogs.'

'I could have told you that and not spent a penny,' Garrett said. 'What else have you got?'

'It's a punishment squad, all right. It must be something special because they appear to be working independently.'

'And?'

Danny nodded. 'It's Hennessy, all right.'

'It's not a surprise, Danny. Any ideas where he's operating out of?'

'Aye. The word is Donaghadee.'

She said they'd gone to the country club.

Did she ever tell you the name of this place?

I asked her that too, making it sound, you know, as if I didn't believe a word she was saying.

Sure and of course I know, said she. Up on the hills above Donaghadee.

'Whereabouts in Donaghadee?'

'A big old place they use for strategy conferences. Craigthomas House.'

'He's there now?'

'That's what I hear.'

'Is Hennessy down there alone, Danny?'

Danny Flynn shrugged eloquently. 'I wouldn't bet on it,' he said.

Garrett moved off down the path towards the gate in Stranmillis Road; when he looked back a few minutes later Danny had gone. He walked out of the

Botanic Gardens and across Stranmillis Road and let himself into the safe house with the keys Lieutenant Christie had given him. Inside, in a sort of vestibule, another door sealed off the stairs to the first floor; a second door to the right was obviously the entrance to the ground floor flat.

Garrett opened the stairway door and went up two flights of carpeted stairs. A landing ran from the front of the house to the back. At the front was a large living room with two casement windows that looked out over the Botanic Gardens. At the rear were a well-equipped kitchen and bathroom. Between them was a bedroom. The furniture was motel-style, functional and impersonal. There was food in the refrigerator, clean linen in the airing cupboard in the hall.

He picked up the telephone book, found the listing for Patricia Burke and rang her number.

'Mr Garrett,' she said. 'I wondered what had happened to you after . . . the other day.'

'I'm sorry it's taken me so long to ring

184

you,' Garrett said. 'I wanted to thank you for what you did.'

'It was little enough.'

'Do you have a car, Mrs Burke?'

'I do. Why?'

'I wondered if you'd care to drive into town tonight and have dinner with me.'

'Well, I . . . '

'They tell me there's a restaurant called Saints and Scholars that's rather good,' Garrett said. 'Would seven-thirty suit you?'

'I'm not sure I — '

'I'll see you then,' Garrett said. He hung up and went into the bathroom to run a hot bath, humming an old tune. He caught sight of himself in the mirror and grinned.

'Ain't misbehavin',' he said.

* * *

The restaurant was on a corner in the prosperous southern part of Belfast, near Queen's University. Garrett arrived first and was shown to the corner table he had asked for on the telephone. He studied the wine list, which looked as if it was trying to be trendy. He played safe and ordered Bourgogne Aligoté; it came to the table with commendable promptness.

He was pouring a second glass when Patricia Burke came in. She left her coat at the cloakroom and came across to the table. She was wearing an off-white longsleeved silk blouse with a bright red silk scarf thrown loosely around her shoulders, a long, full, dark blue woollen skirt, and leather boots. Her naturally curly hair was loosely brushed away from the forehead; he noticed that although there were streaks of grey showing, she was not vain enough to have it dyed.

The attentive waiter poured some wine into her glass. 'I'm glad you could come,' Garrett said.

She grinned, showing dimples. 'My social calendar isn't what you might call crowded, Mr Garrett,' she told him.

'You surprise me,' he said. 'What would you like to eat?'

She took reading glasses out of her handbag and studied the menu carefully. She looked like a teacher checking someone's homework. Her eyes met his.

'I wish you wouldn't watch me quite so intently, Mr Garrett,' she said. 'It makes me feel . . . uneasy.'

'I'm sorry,' he apologized. 'It's a habit. And call me Charles, please. Have you decided?'

'They have chicken Kiev,' she said. 'Do you think it will be full of butter and garlic and everything I oughtn't to eat?'

'We'll ask them to make sure it is,' he said.

The ever alert young waiter saw his signal and came across to take their order. While they waited for the food, Garrett asked Patricia Burke a question.

'I'm a schoolteacher,' she said. 'Why are you shaking your head?'

'Nothing,' Garrett smiled. 'Just a wayward thought. Where do you teach?'

'At the infant school in Dundonald. Five- to seven-year-olds.'

'You enjoy it.'

'There is nothing in the world like being with young children, Mr Garrett — Charles,' she said. 'When everything else fails, there are the children, there are always the children. They give you back your hope, your faith, everything.'

'For of such is the kingdom of heaven,' Garrett said.

'Are you married, Charles?'

'No,' he said. 'My wife died some years ago.'

'No children?'

'No children.'

'That's sad. A man should have children.'

'I haven't quite given up the idea.'

She smiled. 'Ah,' she said. 'Then there's a lady in your life.'

'There is indeed.'

The waiter brought their food and they were silent as it was served. When the little ceremony was over, she picked up her knife and fork and held them poised above the plate.

'This is the part I love,' she said, cutting into the chicken. She bent forward and smelled the juices oozing from it. 'Mmmm, that looks positively sinful.'

She ate with evident enjoyment, looking around at the other diners from time to time, her large brown eyes lively and shining.

'You'll have to forgive me,' she said. 'I don't eat out very often. I want to remember all this so I can tell everyone at school about it.'

'Do you teach full time?'

'Yes, I do. Why do you ask?'

'I just wondered whether you ever get a day off.'

'I never need one. I live a very quiet life.'

'No . . . attachments?'

She looked up quizzically. 'Why do you ask?'

'When I came to see you the other day, you talked about your husband. You said after he died you swore to set your face against the men of violence.'

'I remember.'

'Then you'll also recall we talked about that country club Seamus Arnot and his wife went to?'

'In Donaghadee.'

'It's not a club, Patricia. It's an IRA safe house. Do you know what that is?'

'I've heard the phrase.'

'It's a place used for secret meetings. It's called a safe house because the police don't know about it.'

'Is that why Seamus went there?'

'Probably. The men of violence plan their campaigns in such places. In fact, I have information that there may be a group of them there now doing just that.'

'What has that got to do with me?' she asked.

'I need some help,' Garrett said. 'And you're the only person I know that I could ask.'

'What sort of help?'

'This place, this house they're using is a big old mansion up on a hill in private grounds outside Donaghadee. If we put surveillance teams in the vicinity they would be spotted in ten minutes. We would have the same problem in Donaghadee itself. It's only a small place; half a dozen strangers kicking their heels about the place would stick out like sore thumbs. So the ideal infiltration team would be a man and a woman, preferably husband and wife.'

She shook her head, smiling disbelievingly. 'You're not going to ask me what I think you're going to ask me, are you?'

Garrett smiled back. 'Yes, I am,' he said.

11

The following morning, they drove over to Donaghadee in Patricia Burke's little red Fiat It was a clear bright autumn day, with the sky full of clouds being hurried along by a bullying wind. The countryside between Newtownards and the coast was speckled with the small rounded hills the Irish call drumlins; they looked like half potatoes covered with grass. Donaghadee was a little painted seaside town with a large harbour full of pleasure boats and fishing smacks. A fine white lighthouse stood at the far end of the quay. A rath — an old earth-ringed fort which the locals called the Moat — stood on a hillock in the middle of the town, topped by a castellated powder house that had been erected to store explosives when the harbour was being built. The streets had a cluttered, old-world air.

'Well, are you ready?' Garrett said.

'Yes,' she said. 'How about you?'

'You know what you're looking for?'

'Don't worry. If any of the men whose pictures you showed me are there, I'll recognize them.'

'Try to get a good idea of the layout of the house,' Garrett said. 'Where the emergency exits are, corridors with dead ends, windows with balconies, things like that. We'll need to make a map before we send anyone in there.'

'What will you be doing?'

'I'll go in the back way,' he said. 'Check the perimeter for alarms. What time's your appointment?'

'Two o'clock.'

'Let's get moving,' Garrett said, getting up. 'I want to find a public call box. There's one a little way up Morey Hill.'

'But there's a telephone here in the hotel,' she protested.

He shook his head. Like most civilians, she evinced a touching faith in the sanctity of the phone system. He did not share it. The only secure line was a public telephone, because nobody knew you were going to use it.

The wind blustered at them as they

drove along the seafront. The tide was out now and the dulse-gatherers with their little sickles were collecting the edible seaweed that grew on the rocks. They dried it in the sun till it turned yellow and crackly; people ate it like candy. It was said to be good for the brain, perhaps because of the iodine in it. A few hundred yards up the gentle hill they came to a public call box Garrett dialled the 0232 area code for Belfast, followed by a seven-figure number.

'You have reached six-six-eight, six-seven-eight-eight,' a disembodied voice said. 'Please contact the operator.'

It was a standard security service cover. The normal reaction of anyone dialling the number in error would be to hang up. Garrett waited, listening to the tiny clicks and hisses that told him the recording equipment was switching on. Then the same mechanical voice spoke again. 'When you hear the signal, input the identification code.'

On the tone, Garrett dialled 3333.

'ID and clearance code, please,' a male voice said.

'Charles Garrett. That's George Alpha Roger Roger Egypt Tango Tango. Clearance code PACT, that's Peter Alpha Charlie Tango.'

'Wait, please.'

He waited; the recording they had just made was being matched with the voice print he had made for the computer at security service liaison headquarters. After a few more moments, the line came alive again.

'You are cleared to Central,' the man said. 'Go ahead.'

'This is an UMBRA priority. Ask Colonel Elkins to ring me back at this number immediately.' He gave the number and hung up, checking the street outside. Pat Burke was in the car, looking straight ahead. Two women stood gossiping in front of a fruiterer's shop. A youngster of about ten wearing a T-shirt that said 'Rory Gallagher' was doing wheelies on a beaten-up BMX bike. The phone rang. He snatched it up.

'Garrett?' It was Elkins. 'Where the hell are you? We've been — '

'Shut up and listen,' Garrett said

urgently. 'I'm at Donaghadee. I've got a lead on Sean Hennessy. My source says he may have some of his unit with him. I'm going to check on it.'

Elkins wasted no time on small talk. 'Give me the exact location.'

'Craigthomas. It's a large house on the A2 above Foreland Point, about half a mile north of Donaghadee. Got it?'

'Got it. Don't move till I get some backup over there.'

'Negative,' Garrett said flatly. 'I'm going over the wall to check the grounds. I've got a civilian checking the inside layout. Your job is to get the whole area sealed off. You understand me, Elkins? Sharpshooters, the works.'

'When do you want them in place?'

Garrett looked at his watch. One thirty-five. 'I'll give you two hours. Everyone in place by three forty-five. We'll go in at four.'

'What about Patterson?'

'You brief him. But make sure he doesn't fly off the handle. Nobody goes in until I give the word.'

'What about the boys in blue?'

'No uniforms, under any circumstances. No sirens, no helicopters, no visible roadblocks, nothing overt.'

'I'll set it up. What's our base of ops?'

'Copelands Hotel in Donaghadee. I'll meet you there. Three forty-five prompt. If for any reason I don't make it, go in anyway. Any questions?'

'Only one,' Elkins said. 'Is it shoot to kill?'

'What do you think?' Garrett replied.

★   ★   ★

The wind coming in off the sea whirled gulls above Garrett's head like scraps of paper. Brilliance danced on the dark blue ocean. In the lee of Copeland Island, a sailing boat leaned away from the wind.

'All set?' he asked Patricia Burke. She nodded, her silence betraying the tension she was feeling.

'You know what you have to do?'

'I know. Don't worry.'

He watched as she drove back down the road toward Donaghadee. She had dropped him at Ballycross, beside the secondary road that ran through Skelly Hill across the moors to Bangor. He stood on the corner long enough to be sure no one had followed him, then walked purposefully up the lane that doglegged northwards up the slight slope. It came to an end in a cul-de-sac a few hundred yards from the rear boundary of Craigthomas House. Facing the turning place at the end of the lane was a small cottage; it looked deserted. He went to the front door and knocked: no reply. Checking there was no one in sight, he went round the side of the house and into the neat little garden, a rectangle of grass maybe sixty feet long, with pretty flowerbeds along both sides and a small kitchen garden at the far end. A rickety fence marked the boundary. About ten yards beyond it, across rough pasture, was the eight-foot-high dry-stone wall surrounding Craigthomas House.

* * *

Patricia Burke stopped the car at the gate and waited while the porter used the intercom to call the house. After a few moments, the gates made a metallic sound as if they had been struck with a stick, then swung open. She drove up the curving drive to the house and parked the car in a slot marked 'Visitors'. The heavy oak door stood ajar; she went into the lobby and across to the reception desk, where a smiling young woman greeted her.

'I've an appointment to see Mr Walton,' she told her. 'My name is Patricia Antrim.'

'If you'll just come this way, Mrs Antrim,' the receptionist said. She led the way across the hall into a large, high ceilinged room. Behind a glass panel was an unmanned PBX switchboard. The young receptionist opened a door and stood back. 'Mrs Antrim,' she announced.

'Ah, Mrs Antrim, do come in.' Hugh Walton was a tall, thin man with receding hair and a long, horsey face. He wore a white coat; the breast pocket held four or five pens, and a stethoscope hung round his neck. He stood up to shake hands. His hand was thin and cold, his smile professional. 'Do sit down. You said on the telephone that you'd like to arrange accommodation for . . . ?'

'My mother,' Patricia said.

'Ah, yes,' Walton said, smiling that same cold smile. He took a fountain pen from his pocket and held it poised above a form. 'I'll just jot down a few particulars. Her full name?'

'Catherine Devane.'

'Age?'

'Sixty-two.'

'Address?'

'She lives in Belfast, but she's staying with me at the moment. Mimosa Cottage, Cairngaver Road, Craigantlet.'

'And what exactly is the nature of her illness?'

'She isn't ill,' Patricia said. 'She fell and broke her hip, and she's not really picked up since. I thought that perhaps if she could convalesce somewhere by the sea for a month or two — I work full time, you see — it might do her good.'

'I'm sure it would,' Walton said, still smiling. 'May I ask you how you heard about this establishment?'

'Mother had her operation in the Royal Belfast,' Patricia said. 'One of the consultants there recommended Craigthomas so I thought I'd come and look it over.'

'Which consultant?'

Patricia shook her head. 'I really don't remember. Is it important?'

'No, no,' Walton said, making a gesture. 'Not at all, not at all. However, I, ah, you do realize that this is not a National Health Service establishment, Mrs Antrim?'

'Money isn't a problem,' Patricia said briskly. 'But I'd like to see the place before I make any decision. Perhaps you can tell me something about your facilities.'

'Of course, of course,' Walton said primly. 'Well, let me see. We offer several types of accommodation. For instance, rooms with sea view cost three hundred, garden view two hundred and fifty, and there are a few doubles at two hundred and twenty.'

'Doubles? You mean sharing?'

'That's right.'

'Would it be possible for me to see the accommodation?'

'Certainly, certainly,' Walton said, coolly jovial. 'I'll ask my assistant, Mrs Walsh, to show you around.' He pushed a button on his intercom. 'Could you come in, please, Jill?'

★   ★   ★

Garrett went into the unlocked garden shed and found a stepladder and a spade; he took both to the wall, using the stepladder as an observation platform from which to ensure that there were no alarm wires or security devices before dropping down lightly inside the grounds of Craigthomas House. He checked the shrubbery carefully for electronic beams or tripwires; once he was sure there were none, he set off in the general direction of the house, the spade on his shoulder. Beneath his left arm he carried a shoulder-holstered 9 mm combat version of the Smith & Wesson M39 automatic pistol fitted with a Guttersnipe sight and carrying seven rounds of Parabellum ammunition. Inside the top of his right-hand boot he had taped a sheathed survival knife with a serrated seven-inch blade. He was wearing a flat peaked cap, a heavy navy blue fisherman's sweater, corduroys and Wellington boots. To any casual observer, he would look like one of the gardeners.

As he drew nearer to the big house, he could see figures moving outside a long, low building with a dovecot on the roof; he knew from his researches at the Ordnance Survey in Stranmillis Court and the Public Records Office in Balmoral Avenue that this was the former stables, now converted to staff quarters. Next to it was a tennis court, with a small bar and changing room, and to the left of that, as he looked at it, a triple garage constructed of stucco-faced breeze block with a pitched shingle roof.

He walked round the side of the garage and along a path fringed with shrubbery, which framed a croquet lawn to the rear of the house. The path led him to a brick building with a concrete roof that looked a bit like a World War Two air-raid shelter; the steady electric hum emanating from it told him it housed the generators which supplied the house with power. Dustbins were ranged against the wall of the building beneath a makeshift roof of corrugated iron.

He could hear the clatter of dishes through the open windows of the kitchens on the north side of the house. To his left, screened by banks of rhododendrons, was a tarmac parking area. There were ten or twelve cars, some with Irish registrations and others with the Z suffix that indicated they were local. Beyond the car park, terraced formal gardens sloped gently down to open pastures bisected by bridle paths. He stood for a moment, indecisive. If he went further, he might encounter someone at the front of the house. He'd try the other side.

⋆　⋆　⋆

Jill Walsh was a pert, birdlike woman with the harrassed air of someone with too much to do and not enough time to do it. Walton introduced her as his assistant.

'Jill will show you anything you want to see, Mrs Antrim,' he said. 'Perhaps you'll pop in and see me before you leave?'

Patricia followed her guide out into the hall and they got into a small lift.

'We'll go to the top and work our way down,' Mrs Walsh told her. Patricia nodded, concentrating on physical details. They emerged on a landing beside the stairwell; three windows facing the lift looked out over the grounds to the sea beyond.

'What a wonderful view,' Patricia said.

'Yes,' Mrs Walsh said, her tone that of someone who has heard the remark ten thousand times. She touched Patricia's elbow, steering her around the lift shaft to the central corridor running the length of the house. 'The accommodation you're interested in is this way.'

The corridor had three doors on either side. Mrs Walsh went into the first one on the left and turned to face Patricia. They were in a neat little sitting room, with a TV in one corner, two armchairs, a low table with magazines on it, and a bookcase full of battered paperbacks. On one wall was a print of Degas ballet dancers.

'As you see, patients have private facilities if they prefer to be alone,' she said. 'There is a day room on the floor below for the more gregarious.'

The whole floor was laid out the same way, she explained. Each of the original bedrooms had been partitioned into so-called 'recuperation units'. Each of these cells contained a bed, a small bedside table, a tiny vanitory unit, a small colour TV and a wall-mounted bookshelf.

'Are all the units the same?' Patricia asked, going to the window. She could see the rooftops of Donaghadee and the tapering white finger of the lighthouse at the end of South Pier.

'On this floor, yes,' was the reply.

'What about the front of the house?' Patricia asked.

She thought the woman hesitated, but she could not be sure. 'The suites at the front of the house are being refurbished at present,' Mrs Walsh said. 'Neither will be available for some time.'

'And you say one of these units costs . . . ?'

'Three hundred pounds a week. As you see, all the rooms on this side of the house have a fine view out over the sea.'

'And the other side?'

'They're basically the same except they look out over the gardens. Do you want to see one?'

'I don't think so. What about down-stairs?'

'We can go down and have a look,' Mrs Walsh said. They went back along the corridor to the wide staircase. As they reached it, the door of the private suite on the right opened. Patricia heard the sound of male voices raised in argument and smelled the sharp tang of tobacco smoke. The man who had opened the door stared at her for a moment, then went back into the room, but not before Patricia saw that he was short and sturdily built, with carroty red hair and bright blue eyes. She remembered his face: he was one of the men who'd visited Seamus Arnot. Garrett had told her his name. Hennessy, that was it. Sean Hennessy.

'Who was that?' she asked, hoping that

the shock of recognition had not shown on her face.

'Just a member of staff,' Mrs Walsh said, steering her firmly downstairs. They descended to another landing and walked along the brightly lit corridor. As on the floor above, the original eight bedrooms had been converted to 'recuperation units', but on this floor the spaces occupied by the two mysterious 'suites' above were used on one side as a bathroom and dispensary and on the other as a day room. The sound of a TV game show came from the latter; four men and a woman sitting in a wheelchair with her leg in plaster were watching someone trying to win a microwave oven. All of them were in their mid-thirties or early forties. They did not speak as Patricia came in. The woman was about Patricia's age, with dark hair and truculent eyes that met Patricia's as much as to say, *Who are you looking at?*

★ ★ ★

Garrett retraced his steps to a staircase that led down into a sunken walled garden. Bees hummed lazily among the flowers. The scent of herbs lay musky on the air. He could see an elderly man reading a newspaper in the conservatory. That seemed to be about it. He had a pretty clear picture of the layout for briefing the E4 Ops team. He followed a path that wound among the shrubbery in the formal gardens, terraced on this side as on the other. From this vantage point he had a clear view of the pool, the fieldstone patio and the windows of the conference room behind it. The windows were open and the room appeared to be empty. He looked up at the blank windows of the upstairs floors.

Where are you, Hennessy?

* * *

'Is there anything else you want to know, Mrs Antrim?' Mrs Walsh asked, looking at her wristwatch. 'Anything else you'd like to see?'

'No, I don't think so,' Patricia said. 'Everything seems very clean and well organized.'

'We pride ourselves on that here at Craigthomas,' Mrs Walsh told her. 'Let's go back down to the ground floor and I'll give you a quick tour of the rest of the house.'

Patricia followed her dutifully, nodding approval of the dining room and the library, the conservatory and the swimming pool, smiling at the patients sitting around, some of them in day clothes, others in towelling dressing gowns. There was only one woman, quite elderly; all the rest were men in their mid-twenties or early thirties. One or two of them had aluminium crutches beside their chairs. They looked dispirited and bored, with the lacklustre eyes of refugees. As Mrs Walsh led the way back towards the entrance hall, Patricia asked where the double doors on their right led to.

'The conference room,' Mrs Walsh told her briskly, making no attempt to show it to her. 'It's mostly used for staff meetings. I'll tell Mr Walton we're back. Wait here, please.'

After a minute or two, Hugh Walton

came out of his office, smiling as edgily as before.

'Well, Mrs Antrim,' he said, rubbing his hands together, 'has our Jill taken good care of you?'

'Thank you, I'm very grateful,' Patricia said. 'Of course, as I mentioned earlier, I'll have to talk this over with my husband.'

'Of course, of course,' Walton said. 'And if he wants to come and see the place for himself, just give me a call and we'll fix it up. I'll give you my card. You've got all the brochures and other information?'

'Mrs Walsh already gave them to me.'

'Good, good,' Walton said. He looked nervous, and she wondered why. 'Then . . . you'll forgive me? So much to do, you understand.'

'Of course,' Patricia said. 'I'll see myself out.'

She went out into the hall; the reception desk was empty. There was no sign of anyone. Patricia shrugged and went out through the big oak door into the sunshine. The man she had seen upstairs was standing by her car. She felt the shock of fear inside her body, as tangible as a blow. Hennessy smiled forgivingly at her, as one might smile at a child who has been foolish rather than naughty.

'Well, now, Mrs Burke,' he said. 'Not dashing away, are you?'

★ ★ ★

Garrett went back down the steps into the walled garden and up the other side. He could see the red roof of the old stables above the bushes. He walked north towards the garage block, ready to duck into the shrubbery if anyone appeared. There was no one about. He checked the garages. There was a Ford Transit in one, a Volkswagen microbus in the second, and a powerful-looking Mercedes 300 SEL in the third. He made a note of the registration numbers then checked his watch: time to move out. As he turned, two men came round the corner of the path. Both of them had AR-18 Sterling Armalite 5.56 mm automatic rifles at port on slings round their shoulders.

They saw him an instant after he saw them, but that instant gave Garrett enough time to swing the spade in a short, vicious arc that ended above the ear of the man on the right. The spade made a metallic *bong* as it struck bone. The man cried out in pain, reeling to one side and colliding with his partner. Before either of them could recover, Garrett was on them with a tigerish bound, the wicked survival knife coming up in a short, ugly thrust. The nearer of the two men made a ghastly sound and fell backwards in a thrashing heap, both hands gripping the haft of the deadly weapon that had torn his heart apart.

Garrett was already turning, his hand on the butt of the ASP holstered beneath his left arm. The man he had hit with the spade was getting up, shaking his head, trying to reorient himself. Blood oozed from a deep cut in his scalp just above the right ear. He saw Garrett and sentience came back into his eyes. He tried to pull the Armalite round to a firing position, and he died thinking he had made it. His finger was actually on the trigger when Garrett put a bullet through his brain from the silenced automatic. The man collapsed like a dropped sack, the Armalite clattering on the path. Poised in a halfcrouch, Garrett looked around warily. The brief flurry of bloody violence had taken but a few seconds; no one seemed to have heard or seen it happen.

He dragged the two dead men off the path and hid them as best he could in the thick shrubbery, then turned and ran fast, crouching, between the garage and the tennis court to the rear perimeter wall over which he had entered the grounds. In another ten minutes he was at the Manor Farm crossroads, and in ten more back at the Copelands Hotel in Donaghadee. The little square was busy with shoppers and a few late-season tourists coming back from the Commons, the coastal walk to the south of the town. He looked at his watch again: if everything had gone according to plan, Patricia Burke would already be on her way down from Craigthomas. As soon as she arrived, the operation could move into its next phase.

He leaned against the stone wall, feeling the thin warmth of the October sunshine. He tried to relax. Fat chance.

* * *

'You said there'd be no killing!'

The speaker was Hugh Walton. He paced up and down the room, wringing his hands, his thin face twisted and distraught. 'You promised me there'd be no killing!'

Hennessy looked at Michael Conlan. 'Can you believe this?' he gritted. He turned on Walton in fury. 'Those are our people dead out there, you little fart!'

'Don't you dare to speak to me in that manner!' Walton protested. 'I refuse to allow you to compromise our operation here without written authority from the very top. Do you understand me?'

'Watch out, Sean,' said Jimmy Bounden, sitting to Conlan's right. 'He'll hit you with his vanity case. He'll smack you with his manicure kit.' The men around the table laughed coarsely. As Walton glared at them, Hennessy looked at him with vast pity.

'As of now your operation, as you call it, is finished,' he said harshly. 'Garrett has called a strike. At four, every fucking security organization in Ulster will be coming through that gate down there.'

He looked at the clock. Almost three.

'I made a phone call,' he said, addressing all of them. 'Our men at Stormont confirms what the woman told us. Garrett sent her in to look the place over while he came over the back wall and checked the grounds. It was him killed Bob Povah and Georgie Steele.'

'What do we do now?'

'We get gone,' Hennessy said, 'and fast. They're going to put a ring round this place tighter than a hog's arse in flytime.'

'Where are we going?' Jimmy Bounden wanted to know.

'Johnny Riley's place,' Hennessy said. 'Wateresk Hill.'

Wateresk Hill was an isolated farm up in the hilly countryside above Dundrum Bay, perhaps two miles from the town of

216

Newcastle, itself about thirty miles south by road from Donaghadee. They'd be safe as houses there.

'All of us?'

'That's right. Michael, you and the boys take the Kombi and move out now. Use back roads. I'll follow as soon as I get done here.'

'What about the woman?' Conlan asked.

Hennessy smiled. 'I'll take care of her,' he said.

'And what about me?' Hugh Walton said shrilly. 'What about me?'

Hennessy looked at him with empty eyes. 'Who gives a fuck about you?' he said contemptuously.

12

After his men were gone, Hennessy walked across to the window. The roofs of Donaghadee shone in the afternoon sunshine. The fields were picture-postcard green. The dark sea looked as if someone had sprinkled it with stardust. The wound in his hip throbbed as if in synch with his thoughts. In his mind's eye he saw again the junction at Vinegar Hill, the bright June sun shining, Paddy McCaffery and Garrett up there behind the Land Rover, everything looking good. Diana looked at him, her eyes searching his.

Will I ever see you again?

No. Never.

He remembered how he let go of her arms and gave her a push. She turned her head to look back at him and then started walking. He saw Garrett staring at her, and then at him, and he thought, *Yes, you bastard, I had her*. And then Paddy's head blew apart in a red mist and he heard the spiteful crack of a sniper's rifle. Rage consumed him. He came round the side of the Ford van, firing the Kalashnikov, realizing in the same instant that Diana Garrett was between him and Garrett as she ran across the road but then —

He turned round as the door opened. It was May Nolan. She was wearing a dark blue swimsuit with a thick tan bath towel thrown over her shoulders like a cape. Water dripped from her crotch on to the carpet.

'Enjoy your swim?'

She shrugged. 'It was all right.' Her voice was soft, with a trace of Donegal in it.

'You heard? About Garrett?'

'Michael told me before he left.'

'He's to be outside the Copelands Hotel in Warren Road between three forty-five and four o'clock this afternoon.'

'You're sure?'

'I have it from what they call an impeccable source.'

She smiled the predatory smile of a hunting cat, her mouth firm and full.

'Well, now,' she said. 'That's obliging of him. There I thought I was going to have to go out hunting him. And here he turns up on the doorstep. I'd better get ready to go down to town.'

He looked at her small, slender body and sturdy legs for a moment without speaking. 'Don't be too sure of yourself, May,' he said. 'Don't underestimate this man.'

'Michael told me. About Povah and Steele. He must be very fast.'

'He's that, all right.'

'How did he find this place?'

'Treachery,' Hennessy said softly, holding in the anger. 'And always where you expect it least. Tony Burke's wife, by Jesus!'

'Who is Tony Burke?'

'Was,' he corrected her. 'Tony Burke was a patriot and a martyr who died for the cause ten years and more ago.'

'And what has his wife to do with this?'

'She came here claiming her name was Antrim, pretending she wanted a room for her mother. I recognized her the minute I saw her, and I knew Garrett must have sent her. I never thought he'd use her for cover.'

'You think that's what he did?'

'We've two men dead to prove it.'

'What will you do now?'

'Get done what needs to be done. Then get gone.'

She smiled. 'I'd better get started, then.'

He nodded. 'Is there anything you need?'

'Is the car in place?' He nodded, and she touched his cheek. 'That's all, then. You know how I work.'

'I know.'

'He'll go down, Sean, never fear.'

'I just wish I could be there to see it when he does,' he said fiercely. 'But my face is too well known for me to walk the streets of Donaghadee this day.'

She put her hand on his forearm. 'Hush, now,' she said softly. 'I'll take care of it.'

He let out his breath in a long sigh. 'Be careful, May.'

She smiled. Her dark brown eyes looked almost black beneath the emphatic

221

brows. 'When was I not?'

She padded barefoot out of the room, leaving two dark wet footprints where she had stood. She crossed the hall, feeling the weight of his gaze on her back, and went into the suite on the opposite corner of the house. It was comfortably furnished in traditional country style, with an *en suite* bathroom. She went into the bathroom, stripped off the swimsuit, got into the shower and turned it on, throwing back her head and let the water course between her breasts and down her belly, soaping her strong, firm body. She heard the bathroom door open; a dark shape loomed outside the shower stall.

'You mad bastard!' she smiled, as Hennessy slid back the glass door. 'There's no time for this!'

'I'll be quick,' he said, as he got naked into the shower.

★   ★   ★

'We can't wait much longer, Garrett.'

The speaker was Stephen Elkins. He was pacing up and down in front of the window of the hotel, looking at the busy street outside. Garrett looked at his watch. Three-fifty.

'No sign of Mrs Burke?'

'The watchers report no movement at all up there.'

'Something's wrong,' Garrett said. 'She would have been back long before this.' He turned to Elkins. 'Are your people all in place?'

'Just waiting for the word to move.'

'Where's Patterson?'

'Outside. He hates being cooped up.'

Garrett went outside. Major Patterson was leaning against the wall, watching the traffic. The blue glasses glinted in the thin sunshine. He looked up as Garrett appeared.

'We're wasting our time, you know,' he said bitterly. 'The birds have flown. Probably taken your lady friend with them.'

'You think they've had a tip-off?'

'Too fucking right they have! And you know who they got it from, that public-school prick in there!'

'Where are your sharpshooters?'

Patterson took a large-scale Ordnance Survey map out of his coat pocket. 'X marks the spots,' he said. 'Two here, opposite the main gate, the rest posted at hundred-yard intervals all round the perimeter wall. If anybody was going to try and make a break for it, he'd be dead.'

'But you don't think anybody will?'

Patterson shook his head. 'I told you. We're going to go into that place like fucking gangbusters, and there's going to be nobody there except a couple of invalids. Why didn't you come direct to me instead of giving this take to Elkins, Garrett?'

'And if I had?'

'I'd have kept him out of it. And maybe we would have had a chance at Hennessy and his gang. As it is . . . ' He shrugged. 'It's almost four. We can't wait any longer for Mrs Burke. We either have to move in or pull our people out.'

'We'll move. Pass the word to Elkins, will you?'

'Be right back,' Patterson said, and went into the hotel. Garrett stood in the sunshine, watching the changing light on the sea. A man was gutting fish in a boat down in the harbour. Gulls clamoured above him, wheeling and diving, their *glou-glou* cries thin in the pushing wind. He looked at his watch again. Four o'clock. Where was Patricia Burke?

★ ★ ★

Mary Margaret Nolan was born on 5 May 1963, in a cottage that stood in the shadow of O'Connell Castle at Ballyshannon in southern Donegal. She was not yet twelve years old when her father, Billy Nolan, was shot dead at a farmhouse in County Fermanagh by a UDR 'dirty tricks' unit, a gang of extreme loyalists who riddled his car with more than a hundred bullets and then set fire to it. Alone of her family, May Nolan declared a war of vengeance. By the time she was fourteen, she was already acting as a spotter for the army, and she had graduated from watching the movements of the military to carrying weapons and ammunition long before she left school.

Her three O levels enabled her to get a

job as a counter clerk in a building society in Bundoran. Two years later she set it up for an IRA hold-up that netted more than £75,000; shortly afterwards, as police attention focused on her, she went underground. By the time another two years had passed, the one-time building society clerk had become a ferocious killer; they gave her the name the Banshee because after every kill she disappeared like a ghost.

Well-spoken, respectable-looking, intelligent and without scruple, she became one of the IRA's most valuable secret weapons. There were so many places a woman could go in Ulster that a man could not, especially a good-looking woman like May. She was given all the difficult hits, the close-in assassinations that were the only way to take out well-protected targets, supergrasses and ultraloyalists, RUC traitors and undercover infiltrators. She shot as well as any man. They said that only Death could stop her, and even he was afraid of her.

★   ★   ★

Most shooters used an automatic weapon for firepower, but May preferred a revolver because it was less likely to jam. This particular model was an Agent Model D4 Colt .38 Special with a two-inch barrel, small — only 6¾ inches from muzzle to butt — and light, weighing about fourteen ounces unloaded. For all that, it delivered a respectable 770 fps muzzle velocity, which was more than enough gun for close-range work.

When she was ready, she went downstairs to the basement of the big house and into the long tunnel that had been dug soon after the IRA bought the house, so that those who wished to could leave Craigthomas without being observed. It ran almost due southwest, emerging more than three hundred yards away in a cottage in a cul-de-sac overlooking Skelly Hill Golf Club.

May looked at her watch as she left the cottage: three-fifty. Very good, she thought. She walked down the doglegged lane to the main road and from there into town. Several unmarked cars passed her, heading towards Craigthomas at high speed, big men sitting in the front and the back, their faces blank. She smiled to herself. Motherfuckers.

She reached her destination a few minutes before four o'clock. She schooled herself to calm. This was at once the easiest and the hardest part of what she did. Walking up to the target, putting them in, that was easy; walking — not running — away as if what had just happened did not concern her was the most difficult thing in the world to do, no matter how many times she had done it. Every instinct screamed at her to flee; but if she fled, she knew she was finished. Nobody ever ran in Northern Ireland.

She came into the little square fronting the harbour and as she crossed the street she saw Charles Garrett standing in front of the hotel. He was a big man, easily recognizable: she had seen photographs of that craggy face many times in Hennessy's dossier. He glanced at his watch, then stood waiting. May recrossed the street so that now she was on the same side as he, perhaps sixty yards west of where he was standing.

She put her hand beneath the anorak, feeling the hard, cold certainty of the revolver in the waistband of her Levis. She was ice-cool, hyper-alert. She heard, smelled, felt, saw everything — sparrows quarrelling over a scrap of bread on a wall, the salt tang of the sea, the querulous wail of a child in a pushchair outside a shop, the throb of her own pulse, the rough surface of the pavement beneath her shoes.

Garrett was wearing a tan anorak over a navy blue sweater, brown cords and suede walking boots. He looked big and hard and strong. It'll probably take two or three to put him down, she thought. She was about forty yards away from him now.

May covered another twenty yards. Her hand was on the butt of the gun when a man came out of the hotel and spoke to Garrett. Damnation! May stopped, hesitating in the manner of someone not sure of which direction to go, but still moving forward. The man was tall and thin. He was wearing a British warm and a narrow-brimmed brown suede hat. He half-turned, and May saw the blue-tinted glasses. Her belly froze: Patterson! In the same instant, Patterson recognized her. His face went stiff with shock and he shouted something. Garrett whirled round, saw May, isolated her.

May whipped the snub-nosed Colt revolver out of her waistband, her feet apart, hands braced in the classic shooter's stance. She fired, but Garrett was already moving. He thrust Patterson aside, using his own impetus to hit the ground, rolling, as May's bullet whacked into a glass sign outside the hotel, bursting it into flickering splinters. Everything seemed to be happening very slowly. Patterson was sprawled on the pavement, his mouth a round O, Garrett on one knee now, a gun in his hand, May turning, moving. Both of them fired, and May thought she saw Garrett flinch. In the same instant something struck her in the chest and she felt the world tilt. She tried to pull the trigger of the Colt again, and then another bullet struck her above the right eye and she was on the ground and she could see the bright blue sky and she wondered, *How?* And then she was dead.

13

White ceiling. Green walls. The smell of
formaldehyde and antiseptic: a hospital.
He remembered the woman coming
towards him, dark hair, dark empty eyes
beneath knitted brows, the little yellow
flower of flame from the muzzle of the
pistol.

'Feeling better?'

A young nurse was standing beside his
bed, smiling. He tried for a snappy reply,
but couldn't think of one; he decided to
leave it until later.

'Where is this?' he asked her.

'The Army hospital,' she said. 'Belfast.'

'What happened . . . at Donaghadee?'

'I don't know anything about Donaghadee,' she said. 'All I know is you were
shot.'

'What about the woman?'

'What woman would that be?'

'Never mind.'

As he spoke, the door opened and a

young doctor in surgical greens came in. He was compactly built, with dark curly hair and horn-rimmed glasses. When he smiled he had dimples that would have made a debutante jealous. His name tag identified him as John Cosgrove. The young nurse smiled at him in that smitten way nurses often smile at handsome young doctors, and went out, closing the door quietly behind her.

'Well, well, Mr Garrett,' Cosgrove said. 'Back to the land of the living, eh?'

'Sort of.'

'You're a lucky fellow, my friend,' the doctor said. 'A few more inches to the right, and . . . *zzzzck*.' He made a throat-slitting gesture. 'As it is, you've got a nasty wound under your right arm and a cracked rib.'

'In my line of business, a miss is a lot better than a mile,' Garrett told him. 'Can I get up?'

The doctor looked at him and smiled. 'Certainly,' he said cheerfully. 'Go right ahead. You'll start bleeding the minute you do, of course. But yes, get up, by all means.'

'How about that?' Garrett said, managing a faint grin this time. 'A doctor with a sense of humour.'

'You need one in this place, laddie,' Cosgrove said. 'Don't worry, we'll have you out of here by tomorrow: we need the space for people who are really hurt. Now: do you feel up to seeing visitors?'

'Let me guess,' Garrett said. 'Colonel Elkins? Major Patterson?'

'Right both times.'

'As you said, doctor, I'm a lucky fellow. I don't suppose you could persuade them to come back another time? Say about four years from now?'

Cosgrove grinned and opened the door. The two security officers came in, and Elkins held the door open, waiting pointedly until Cosgrove got the message and left. Closing the door firmly behind him, Elkins hitched his rump on to the rounded end of the iron bedstead. Patterson looked around, and then sat down in the bentwood chair provided for visitors.

'How are you feeling?' he asked.

'Like a nightingale without a song to

sing,' Garrett said. 'Are you waiting to see how long it will be before I explode with suppressed curiosity, or are you going to tell me what happened at Craigthomas?'

'Hell, that's easy enough,' Patterson said disgustedly. 'Nothing happened. The bastards were gone. Vanished. Pffft.'

'What about Patricia Burke?'

'No sign of her,' Elkins interposed. 'She's missing. We found her car parked in a space outside the house, so we have to assume they took her with them.'

'How the hell did they get clear?' Garrett said angrily. 'I thought you had the place sewn up tight!'

'Just a minute, Garrett,' Patterson said, bridling. 'My people were told to take no action until they got the go-ahead from you. They were still waiting when you met up with the little lady with the gun.'

'Ah, yes, the little lady with the gun. Tell me about her.'

'Her name was Mary Margaret Nolan.'

'Was?'

'You hit her just above the heart,' Elkins told him. 'Patterson put one through her head. Either would have killed her.'

'Mary Margaret Nolan,' Patterson repeated. 'Better-known as the Banshee. We wanted her in connection with a dozen different sectarian killings.'

'Why did she come after me?'

'That's a silly question,' Patterson said. 'To kill you, of course.'

'He doesn't mean why, Harry,' Elkins explained patiently. 'He means *why*?'

Patterson looked baffled, which seemed to be what Elkins had intended. 'My guess would be they sent her after you to take the heat off them while they got clear of Craighthomas.'

'Let's accept the possibility. What happened after I got shot?'

'The manure hit the air-conditioning,' Elkins said, with a shrug. 'We knew we were blown, so we went straight in and kicked the doors down.'

'There was nobody home, you said.'

'Nobody we wanted,' Patterson said. 'Oh, we picked up a couple of small-time villains, including the fellow who runs the place, one of those doctors with no qualifications, name of Hugh Walton, and his assistant, a woman called Walsh. We'll put them through the mincer, but I doubt they'll tell us anything of value.'

'We found a tunnel in the cellar,' Elkins added. 'Professional job, probably done by local quarry miners. Shored up, reinforced, the business. It runs from the big house to a cottage on Skelly Hill Lane. They probably had cars waiting there. If not, all they had to do was walk down the street and catch a bus. They were probably long gone by the time we went in.'

'What time were our people in place?'

'Surveillance teams, three thirty-five. Shooters on the perimeter walls ten minutes later.'

'So Hennessy and his people must have been out of there before three-thirty.'

'The manager, Walton, said seven of them left in a VW Kombi. Hennessy and the Burke woman were in a Mercedes.'

'We ran the vehicles through PDVC. The Merc had never even been stopped at a road check.'

'Is anybody prepared to guess where

they might have gone?'

'Into deep cover,' Elkins said gloomily. 'They wouldn't cross into the Republic in case we had watchers out. They're in a safe house somewhere right now, drinking Bushmills and laughing themselves sick.'

'Why did they take Mrs Burke?'

'There can only be one reason. She might come in useful. If not, they'll get rid of her.'

'Now we come to the big question,' Garrett said. 'How did they know we were coming?'

'As you might imagine, the DCI asked much the same question.' The Director and Co-ordinator of Intelligence headed what was known as the Department at Stormont; although the Chief Constable, RUC, and the General Officer Commanding armed forces were nominally independent, in fact every arm of the security services in Northern Ireland reported to him. No newspaper ever printed his name, no radio or TV programme even mentioned his existence.

'And what did you tell him?'

Elkins glared at Patterson. 'I told him

someone tipped them off,' he said. 'It's the only explanation.'

'It begins to look as if you're right,' Garrett said.

'Of course I'm right,' Elkins said angrily. 'There was a bloody leak, and we all know where it came from!'

'You're so fucking anxious to pin it on me, aren't you, Elkins!' Patterson snapped, balling his fists and getting to his feet. 'You did at the DCI's inquest and you're still doing it.'

'If the cap fits,' Elkins snapped back.

Garrett held up a hand to stop the squabble. 'What was the DCI's verdict at the after-action meeting?'

Elkins shrugged. 'You know the DCI, Garrett. He's a politician, not a field man. He's got one eye on his job and the other on his knighthood. If he calls in Internal Affairs, it will go into the file. He doesn't want an inquiry. So he wants it sorted out quickly. He's given us an ultimatum: one month to clean house.'

'And can you do it?' Garrett was looking at Patterson as he spoke, but it was Elkins who answered.

'I told him if he'd give me *carte blanche* I'd nail the bastard in a week,' he said aggressively.

Patterson shook his head like a goaded animal. 'You don't believe this shit, do you, Garrett?'

'I'll be out of here tomorrow,' Garrett said, avoiding a direct reply. 'When I arrive at the castle, I want a complete breakdown of the Craigthomas operation waiting for me. I want a secure room with a computer, fax and phone. I want the intimate details, gentlemen. Who was there, who knew about it, who might have known about it. I want the duty rosters and the movement dockets, firearms releases, vehicle requisitions — the works.'

'Is that all?' Elkins said, with a little disbelieving laugh.

'You once told me you'd check up to see how much clout PACT has,' Garrett told him. 'Do you want to really find out?'

Elkins stared at him defiantly. Garrett waited. He knew what was going through the other man's head. Elkins had some clout himself: his father was very near the top of the tree in the office of the Co-ordinator of Intelligence.

'Take your best shot, Elkins,' Garrett said. 'And I'll take mine.'

Elkins looked at him for a long moment, and then at Patterson. 'You wouldn't be taking sides, would you, Garrett?' he said softly.

Garrett shook his head. 'Even if I had the inclination, I don't have the time. I'm only interested in finding Patricia Burke and taking Hennessy out of circulation. Preferably, but not necessarily, in that order.'

Elkins got up and put on his overcoat. His face was stiff. All right, it said. If that's the way you want it.

'Tomorrow, then,' he said, and went out.

Patterson grinned.

'You mind if I tell you something, Garrett?'

'Go ahead.'

'When you first arrived here, I thought you were just another of those London idiots they keep sending over here. Now that I know you better, I realize you're not even that smart. If you can't see that Elkins is a bad apple, you don't belong in this racket.'

'God,' Garrett said. 'You're lovely when you're angry.'

Patterson's fists clenched and he took a step towards the bed. The young doctor stepped between him and Garrett.

'Out,' Cosgrove said, emphasizing the order with a jerk of the thumb.

'I'm not through here.'

'Wrong,' Cosgrove said. 'Out!'

Patterson glared at him for a moment longer, and then got control of himself. 'You remember what I said, Garrett,' he hissed, then turned and wrenched the door open, slamming it behind him. John Cosgrove's sigh was audible in the silence that followed. Garrett grinned.

'I think I could use you in my organization, doctor,' he said. 'You interested?'

'I like my body the way it is, thanks,' Cosgrove told him. 'No bullet holes, no vital parts missing. You boys play too rough for me.'

'It's a rough game,' Garrett said.

14

Two days of intensive backtracking across every aspect of the Craigthomas operation gave Garrett nothing but eyestrain. The dredgers reported that Hugh Walton, former administrative manager of the Craigthomas operation, was much more frightened of the IRA vengeance than he was of any threats they made. It was going to take time to break him down, and time was one thing Garrett didn't have a lot of. He decided to get back on the street; apart from anything else, the atmosphere inside NIHQ was so poisonous that he felt the need of some fresh air.

Failures like the Craigthomas raid only exacerbated the discontent; as a result of it, Elkins was acting like a sulky schoolboy and Patterson had simply locked himself away, leaving Christie to answer all queries. Garrett didn't allow himself to be angered.

He checked out of the security enclave

and drove down to the centre of Belfast. He left the car in the car park between the bus station and the old cattle market and walked west through the city centre, past City Hall and towards the Royal Belfast Academic Institution, or 'the Inst', as locals called it.

At the end of Howard Street he turned left into Great Victoria Street, past the New Vic and the Opera House, and went into the Crown where he stood at the bar with a half-pint of draught Guinness.

'Could you manage another of those, sor?'

He looked up to see Danny Flynn standing beside him 'Don't mind if I do,' Garrett said. 'How are you, Danny?'

The Irishman grinned and signalled for two more glasses of Guinness, which Dubliners would tell you was made from the water of the River Liffey. But then, Dubliners would tell you anything if it made a good story.

'Didn't keep you waiting long, did I?'

Garrett shook his head as Danny raised his glass. '*Slàinte*!'

As usual, Danny looked as if he had

stepped out of a fifties clothing ad. Today he was wearing a Harris tweed hacking jacket with a centre vent, brown cavalry twill trousers, a checked woollen shirt with a narrow knitted tie, and a suede cap. Garrett made himself a bet and glanced down: yes, suede boots with crepe soles, the kind they used to call brothel-creepers.

'You've missed our meet a few times,' Danny observed. 'At the sassafras tree.'

'I was unavoidably detained,' Garrett told him.

'Come on, Danny, drink up and let's take a walk.'

They strolled over to the Queen Street security barrier and turned north into the Cornmarket.

'Your information on Hennessy was good, Danny,' Garrett said as they walked. 'He was right where you said he would be.'

'I'm glad to hear it,' Danny said. 'Do I take it you have the man under lock and key now?'

Garrett shook his head. 'He gave us the slip. We lost him.'

'Ah,' Danny said. He was silent for a

while. 'There was nothing in the papers about Donaghadee. I looked, special,' he remarked.

'I stuck a D-notice on it,' Garrett explained. D-notices prevented the press from reporting matters which were secret or of special security interest by the government. Danny knew the jargon.

'Would you be able to tell me what happened?' he asked.

Garrett gave him an edited outline of events at Craigthomas from the time Patricia Burke had gone in through the front entrance, saying nothing about his own activities.

'The more you tell me, the more it sounds like they knew what you were up to, Mr Garrett.'

'I'm inclined to agree,' Garrett said. 'Hennessy certainly knew where I was. He sent someone after me. A woman named Mary Margaret Nolan.'

Danny Flynn whistled between his teeth. 'I've heard a lot about that one,' he said. 'And none of it good.'

'You won't be hearing about her any more.'

'The fact that I'm talking to you tells me that, Mr Garrett,' Danny said. 'Not many walked away from meeting the Banshee.'

'I was hoping to keep the body count down, Danny. Instead of which, it keeps getting bigger.'

'That was the impression I got from . . . certain people,' Danny said. 'He always was a wild one, Hennessy. It could be he's out of control.'

'What would they do in that situation, Danny? Would they take him out?'

Danny shook his head. 'They rarely take disciplinary action, Mr Garrett. You know that. They might say they have. More likely they'd make an announcement, disown him publicly to placate people in advance, but let him run.'

'That's what I was afraid of,' Garrett said. 'You see, when Hennessy did a runner, he took Mrs Burke with him.'

'This Mrs Burke: I take it she's important to you, Mr Garrett?'

Garrett smiled. 'Not the way you mean, Danny. But I put her at risk. That makes it my fault, mine alone. I've got to find out where she is.'

Danny frowned and stopped to look at a display advertising the forthcoming Ulster Antiques and Fine Art Fair in a shop window.

'It won't be easy, Mr Garrett. You know how it is. You can't ask too many questions about the same people.'

'If I had some other names . . . '

'That was what I was bringing you, Mr Garrett,' Danny said. 'I've got a couple of names. The word is they're part of Hennessy's unit. I've writ them down for you.'

He handed Garrett the packet of Rizla cigarette papers. Garrett took out the top one and read it by the light on the window illuminations. 'Michael Conlan, James Bounden. Peter Nash. Is that all?'

'What did you expect?' Danny said irritably. 'Miracles?'

'Sorry, Danny,' Garrett said. 'I'll put them through the mincer. They may give us some sort of lead. God knows, we need one.'

He handed the cigarette papers back to Danny, who took one out and used his little machine to roll a cigarette with it. He then put the cigarette into his mouth and lit it.

'What can you tell me about the woman?' he asked.

'Full name Patricia Mary Burke. Age thirty-eight. She's a teacher, lives at Craigantlet. She was married to one of the boys. His name was Antony Burke. He was killed when Paddy McCaffery was taken at Portnoo back in — '

'I remember when,' Danny said. 'Sure, there's women still put flowers on Paddy's grave on the anniversary of that day.'

'She was supposed to come back down to Donaghadee after she got through at Craigthomas, but she never turned up. We found her car, but they'd taken her with them.'

'Would there be a photograph, by any chance?'

Garrett shook his head. Danny shrugged fatalistically, watching Garrett with shrewd eyes.

'I'll need some more grease, Mr Garrett,' Danny said. 'A few hundred. Have your people got any idea at all where the boys could be hiding?'

'We've already turned over half a hundred drums, Danny,' Garrett told him. 'Every safe house we know about. If there were still such things as All Points Bulletins, we'd have one out. We've tried everything we know, and so far we've come up empty. Nothing.'

'They could be in the Republic.'

'The woman had no passport.'

'A little thing like that wouldn't bother them. Sure, there's a dozen places you can cross without going through a checkpoint.'

Garrett walked over to the bandstand opposite McManus' shoe shop. He took a bulky nine-by-six manila envelope out of the pocket of his trenchcoat and laid it on the low wall beside him.

'There's another five hundred in there,' he told Danny. 'Even in these times of high inflation that ought to buy something.'

Danny picked up the envelope and stowed it in his pocket. He looked up at the four-faced clock inside its tubular cage at the centre of the precinct.

'Twenty to ten,' he said inconsequentially. 'If I hop to it, I'll be back just in time for the news on TV.'

'Be in touch, Danny,' Garrett said.

'Check the drop in two days and every day after that. Goodnight, Mr Garrett.'

Garrett walked over to the clock tower and sat on the low circular brick surround as the little Ulsterman hurried off towards Victoria Square. As far as he could tell, no one went after him. After a while Garrett got up and set off towards City Hall. He stopped periodically to check for a tail; no one seemed to be particularly interested in him.

He got into the car and drove back to the flat in Stranmillis Road. This was the part he hated most: waiting. He got out a glass bowl, cracked four eggs and a dash of milk into it, and whisked the mixture until it had a foamy head. He put the eggs into the microwave for two minutes, and while they precooked, he made some fresh coffee and cut two slices of brown wholemeal bread. When the microwave pinged, he stirred the eggs and put them back for another minute. Next he put the bread into the toaster; it popped out just far enough ahead of the microwave's second ping for him to butter it and put it on a plate. He grated some fresh pepper and salt on the eggs and ate them standing in the kitchen. It was a long way from cordon bleu cookery, but it was good.

He got up and poured himself another drink and looked at the telephone. It would have been nice to talk to Jessica. He settled for wondering where she was and what she was doing. But it wasn't either his job or hers to entertain the bored security listeners who were sitting up at Security HQ waiting for him to use the phone. He leaned back in the chair. He was asleep in moments.

Someone banged on the door again, once, twice.

'Garrett, are you there?' It was Steve Elkins. Garrett opened the door and Elkins came in, bringing the chill of the October night in with him.

'I was asleep.' Garrett said, looking at his watch. It was four a.m. He shivered. 'What is it?'

'I think we've got something.'

Garrett's tiredness disappeared like smoke. 'Go on.'

'We've located Hennessy's Mercedes. In Newry.'

15

Elkins had a car waiting. A Jaguar XJ6: nothing like keeping a low profile, Garrett thought. He shrugged into his Burberry and jammed the battered Donegal tweed hat on his head. They hurried out into the dawn streets. Streaks of pale grey in the sky heralded the coming morning. The slamming doors sounded like muffled shots.

'Go,' Elkins said to the driver. The sleek black Jaguar slid past the Lyric Theatre and down to the embankment along the river. As they were crossing King's Bridge, Garrett asked a question.

'How many IRA safe houses in Newry?'

'The county? At a guess, forty or fifty. Probably as many again, if not more, that we don't know about. That's bandit country down there.'

'Where was the car? Centre or suburbs?'

'Centre. Near St Patrick's church.'

'Anyone gone near it?'

'No. We're keeping it under surveillance. It's probably been abandoned.'

'No sign of the other vehicle? The VW Kombi?'

'Not yet.'

'Why Newry?'

Elkins shrugged. 'It's on the main A1 road to Dublin. Frontier crossing is just a few miles south. Or they could take a boat from Warrenpoint, sail down Carlingford Lough and on to Dundalk or Dublin.'

'No,' Garrett said emphatically. 'They haven't gone into the Republic.'

'What makes you so sure?'

'It's not the nature of the beast, Elkins. Hennessy has a hostage. He hasn't abandoned her and he hasn't killed her, so that means he must be going to use her for something. He can't do that from Southern Ireland, so he's got to stay in the North. The big question is, where in the North?'

'Wrong,' Elkins said, as they turned off the Upper Newtownards Road into the security enclave. 'The big question is, what's he going to do with the hostage?'

Lights were burning everywhere. An armed soldier checked their passes and waved them through. They got out of the car and hurried upstairs. Phones were ringing. Efficient-looking secretaries bustled along the corridors. They went into Elkins' office.

'Coffee?'

'I thought you'd never ask,' Garrett said. 'Black, one sugar. Have you got a map of Newry?'

'On the desk,' Elkins said, filling the coffee maker. Garrett switched on the desk lamp and stared at the street map. It didn't tell him anything he didn't already know. He walked across to the large-scale map of Northern Ireland on the wall. Newry stood on the river of the same name that widened into Carlingford Lough at Warrenpoint. To the southeast and southwest reared the hills the tourist brochures insisted on calling mountains, although few of them were much more than two thousand feet high: Slieve Gullion, Carlingford, Black Mountain, to the southwest; and to the southeast, the Mountains of Mourne.

Elkins brought the coffee across then went back and sat down behind his desk.

'Did a lot for Ireland, Percy French,' Garrett said.

'Sorry?'

'Percy French. He wrote the song 'The Mountains o' Mourne'. Not to mention 'Phil the Fluter's Ball'.'

'I don't quite — '

'Of course, he missed once in a while,' Garrett went on. ''Oklahoma Rose', for instance. That was a flop.'

'Is there some significance to all this?' Elkins said, sipping his coffee. 'Some point I'm missing?'

Garrett shook his head. 'Forget it,' he said. 'It's just something I do when I'm thinking.'

'Is that a fact?' Elkins said. He put the arch of his handmade shoe against the edge of his desk, tilting back the chair, and took a cigar, one of the kind that have plastic mouthpieces already fitted, from a packet on the desk. He lit it and blew pungent smoke towards the ceiling.

Garrett wondered what he was working up to. He didn't have to wait long to find out.

'How did you know Hennessy was at Donaghadee, Garrett?'

A soft answer turneth away wrath, Garrett decided. 'You forget I was here before you were. I have a few sources.'

'I'd like to know who they are.'

'I'll bet you would,' Garrett said.

'Dammit, Garrett, you can't operate independently! We'll be falling over each other's feet!'

'Then you'll just have to watch your step,' Garrett told him flatly. 'Everything I've learned in the short time I've been in Belfast tells me this place has got more leaks in it than a colander.'

'Are you saying they come from my department?' Elkins asked, spots of colour staining his pudgy cheeks.

'It doesn't make any difference where they're coming from,' Garrett said. 'Until the hole is plugged, I'm not taking any chances.'

'I could require you to reveal your sources, you know,' Elkins said tentatively.

'Under the Prevention of Terrorism Act, I have almost unlimited powers.'

'You mean the DCI has, don't you?'

Elkins smiled. 'Of course,' he said silkily. 'But if I told the DCI you had information which would enable me to expose whoever is passing information from here, he wouldn't squawk if I threw you into the Rathole and left you there to rot.'

'You could try it,' Garrett said levelly. He walked across and stood in front of Elkins' desk, looking the man straight in the eye. 'Do you want to?'

Elkins smiled his smooth smile again and shook his head.

'Back off, then,' Garrett told him.

'I wish you'd trust me, that's all,' Elkins said.

'Who do I contact in Newry?' Garrett asked.

Elkins nodded. 'Dial 0693 followed by 444 and then 818283. Ask for John Pollard.'

Garrett picked up the red phone and dialled the thirteen digits. When Pollard answered he gave his code and asked a question.

'No movement at all, sir,' Pollard said. 'Nobody's come near the vehicle.' He had a Derry accent, his voice rising at the end of each sentence as if it were a question.

'What do the local police say?' Garrett said, signalling to Elkins to pick up the extension.

'They say if it wasn't for us they'd have towed it away long since, sir,' Pollard reported. 'They've had several calls about it from residents already.'

'Give it till mid-morning, John,' Elkins cut in. 'If we get no takers, you'll have to move it.'

'Yes, sir.'

'Send a bomb squad to look it over first,' Garrett reminded him.

'I'll do that, never fear.' They could almost see his smile.

'Where will they take the car?' Garrett asked.

'We've got a secure garage on the industrial estate north of town,' Elkins told him. 'They'll take it apart one screw at a time.'

'I'm going down to Newry,' Garrett said abruptly. 'I want to see that car before anybody touches it.'

'Why?'

'A hunch.'

'I'll come with you.'

'No,' Garrett said. 'There's something I have to do on the way, and I want to be alone when I do it.'

'Thanks,' Elkins said sourly. 'What is it this time, another of your mysterious informants?'

Garrett shook his head. 'You might call it a sentimental journey,' he said.

★ ★ ★

To get where he wanted to go he had to drive maybe sixty miles out of his way; he wasn't even quite sure why he was doing it or who he was doing it for. Maybe it was to remind himself why he was in this business, he decided. That would do for a reason until the real one came along.

It was a junction of minor roads, quite deserted, at a place called Vinegar Hill. He stopped the car and got out, standing near the black and white signpost, its arms pointing the way to Dromore in one direction and Fintona in the other. A soft breeze moved the trees; rooks cawed raucously in their empty branches, and sheep grazed peacefully on the slopes of the nearby hills.

Is it yourself, Garrett?

You know it. Where is my wife?

Did he actually shout, or did he just think he had done so as he ran towards Diana? He saw Hennessy coming out from behind the Ford van. Diana started running. The Kalashnikov assault rifle made an insignificant popping noise and she slewed sideways and all the world stood still.

Sean Hennessy.

A car thief at twelve, a lookout at fourteen, a member of the East Tyrone Brigade by the time he was eighteen. Shrewd, intelligent, capable: a man who figured the odds for and against himself as clinically as a calculating machine, a man who could one moment talk of taking holy orders and the next murder an innocent woman in cold blood. How many times had he almost had him? Four? Six?

We'll settle this one day, Garrett!

Yes, you bastard, he thought, we will.

'Top of the morning to you!'

The voice that interrupted his reverie was loud and cheerful. A portly, red-faced young fellow wearing corduroys, a beaten-up quilted jacket and a flat cap was going by on a bicycle.

'Morning.' The man raised a hand, pedalling strongly up the lane toward Rakeeranbeg Bridge. Garrett allowed himself a wry smile. Only the haunted see the ghosts, he thought, and it's probably just as well, for there are a very great many of them. He got back into the car. There was nothing here any more. Just a road junction, just trees and hills and sheep and the little stream running diagonally across the meadow. What had happened here was gone into the past, a matchstick on a mighty river. Like rowers, we see only the past stretch out before our eyes; the future is always behind us. The Greeks had a word for it but he was damned if he could remember what it was.

He reached Newry just before nine and

headed straight for the centre of the town. When he got to Church Street, a traffic policeman was redirecting motorists round the church. Police cars were parked aslant, radios crackling with incomprehensible squawks. Garrett stopped and a uniformed policeman came across to his car.

'Keep moving, keep moving,' he said impatiently.

Garrett held up his Ministry of Defence ID. The constable's eyes widened.

'John Pollard,' Garrett said brusquely. 'Where is he?'

'Over there, sir,' the policeman said. 'In the dark blue raincoat.'

Beyond the perimeter of blue and white plastic tape stretched across the street, a knot of men were standing near a dark blue Mercedes parked with two wheels on the kerb. Garrett parked his car next to one of the police Granadas and walked over to join them. A tall, grey-haired RUC officer with silver bars on the epaulettes of his raincoat headed to cut him off.

'Now, now, sir, no one's allowed in here,' he said soothingly.

Garrett showed the MoD card again. The police officer's eyes weighed up his car, his clothes and, for all Garrett knew, his inside leg measurements, not missing a thing. It was a pretty safe bet that if someone asked him, he would be able to give a detailed description of Garrett. That was why he was wearing the silver bars. The policeman saluted and stood back, neither impressed nor abashed. 'John Pollard?' Garrett said.

The man in the blue gaberdine raincoat looked round. He was about thirty-five, with a smooth, boyish face and gingery hair. He frowned, automatically cataloguing Garrett's appearance. Some good men on the ground today, Garrett thought, waiting until recognition dawned on the DI5 officer's face.

'Mr Garrett? Good morning, sir.'

He pumped Garrett's hand with the enthusiasm of a man who is not at all unhappy to pass responsibility to someone else. 'Let me introduce you. This is Harold Purcell, our local police liaison officer. Superintendent Colclough, RUC Special Branch. Sergeant Paul Hepton, Bomb Squad.'

'Glad to meet you, gentlemen,' Garrett said. 'What's your assessment, sergeant?'

Hepton had the resigned expression of a man who knows there are more questions than answers. He shrugged.

'I've had a good look underneath her, sir,' he reported in a plangent Liverpool accent. 'She looks clean.'

'Sniffer dogs had a go?'

'Yes, sir. Nothing.'

'We were told to wait till you got here before we opened her up,' Pollard said. Garrett looked over his shoulder; an Army truck was parked just round the corner of the street opposite. On the road beside it was an armoured remote-control robot. It looked like a large lawnmower without handles, squat, featureless and somehow menacing.

'We don't need that thing,' he said flatly. 'The car isn't rigged.'

'With all due respect, Mr Garrett, you can't possibly know that for certain,' Superintendent Colclough said. 'I cannot permit —'

'There's no bomb,' Garrett insisted. 'The people who left this car here did so because they wanted us to find it. Blowing it to pieces would defeat the object of the exercise. Someone get me a set of skeleton keys.'

'Mr Garrett, I repeat, I cannot permit you or anyone else to attempt to open that car. Quite apart from the risk to yourself, the danger to civilian life — '

'Superintendent, if you want to clear the area, you go right ahead and do it,' Garrett said. 'I'll take full responsibility for my own actions. Now: can I have a set of keys?'

The tall officer glared at him for a long moment. Garrett met his angry gaze with equanimity. Both of them knew who had the clout, and if it salved the policeman's pride to balk for a moment or two, that was perfectly acceptable.

'Get him a set of keys,' Colclough rasped to one of his officers. 'Then get everybody off the street. And I mean everybody.'

'Yessir!' The policeman ran across to one of the cars, ran back with a large ring of keys. All police vehicles carry duplicate lock and ignition keys for all but the most unusual marques of car, and this one was no exception. The policeman handed them to Garrett and then ran back to the car; his partner reversed down the street, gears screaming like an enraged bear. Shouted commands bounced off the walls of the houses, and Garrett heard the Army truck start up. In a few minutes he was alone; somewhere he heard the sharp crackle of a transponder, but otherwise he could have been in the Gobi desert.

Well, he thought.

The keys on the six-inch-diameter ring were tabbed: British Leyland, Ford, Vauxhall and so on. There were a dozen or so marked Mercedes, several with the acronymm '300SEL'. He knew '300' meant the car had a three-litre engine, but what did SEL stand for? I'll ask someone later if I'm still around, he decided with gallows humour. He went across to the car and carefully slid one of the keys into the door lock and tried to turn it. No good. He tried another. Nothing. His hands were sweaty. He tried a third key, and this time it turned. The locks sighed open. Now the hard part, he thought. If the car was booby-trapped, opening the door would be the likeliest way to throw the trembler. He felt perspiration trickling down his back. He rubbed his hands together to dry them and then opened the door.

Nothing happened.

Feet pounded on the pavement behind him. First to reach the car was Pollard, closely followed by Superintendent Colclough, and then a whole crowd: soldiers, police, some civilians who hadn't been in evidence earlier. Garrett was already sitting in the driving seat, reading the note he had found taped to the inside of the glove compartment.

'There might be prints on that,' he heard Superintendent Colclough say disapprovingly.

'I know who it's from, super,' he replied.

'What does it say?' The speaker was the young DI5 officer, Pollard. Garrett handed him the scrap of paper.

'See for yourself,' he said harshly, and

got out of the car, pushing past the men clustered around the open door. Pollard read the note out loud.

'A present for Charles Garrett. Look in the boot.' He turned to look at Garrett, who was standing by the rear bumper of the sleek blue vehicle. 'You think it's a trick, Mr Garrett? Could the boot be booby-trapped?'

'No,' Garrett said emptily. He went round to the back of the car and used the same key that had opened the car door to open the boot. A coppery fecal stink filled the air.

'Oh, Jesus,' the sergeant said, clapping his hand over his mouth. Crammed into the boot, his body bent backwards in an obscene arc, was a naked man. Staring green eyes bulged outwards like those of a frog, and his tongue looked like a blackened pork fillet stuck in his mouth. Plasticized clothes line had been looped around his neck in a more or less classic hogtie: simple, foolproof, deadly. Tie the victim's hands behind him, tie them to his feet, then loop his ankles to his neck, maybe even using a knee to get the rope really taut. The victim would keep his muscles tensed as long as he could, but nobody could do it forever. Eventually sheer fatigue would force him to relax and in doing so, strangle himself. Very slowly. Very slowly indeed.

Garrett turned away from the purple-faced corpse, aching with regret.

How's Moira?

Fat and happy.

How many kids now?

Four. And a bun in the oven.

John Pollard came and stood beside him. His face was grey and drawn, as if he had a stomach cramp. He looked at Garrett as if he intended to memorize every feature of the big man's face so that he would never ever forget him.

'You knew, didn't you?' he said angrily.

'No,' Garrett said. 'I expected it would be . . . a message. For me. But not this.'

'Who is it, Garrett?' Superintendent Colclough rasped fiercely. 'Who is that poor sad bastard in the boot?'

'His name is Danny Flynn.'

'A friend of yours?'

'Yes,' Garrett said. 'From Belfast.'

'Belfast? Then how the hell did he get to Newry?'

'I don't know,' Garrett replied thoughtfully. 'But I plan to find out.'

16

John Pollard's department — he had smiled apologetically at the use of the word — occupied a suite of offices in the government buildings on the west bank of the Newry canal.

'Coffee, Mr Garrett.'

John Pollard put the steaming mug on the desk; Garrett turned away from the window. He could feel the other man's eyes watching him speculatively.

'They've taken the Merc to the workshops,' Pollard told him. 'Belfast sent a team down. They'll call us if they find anything.'

'What about Danny Flynn?'

'In the morgue. There'll be an autopsy, of course. Do we release anything to the press?'

'Not before I talk to his wife,' Garrett said, perhaps more harshly than he intended. Pollard flinched visibly.

'Of course,' he said.

'Sorry. I'm not looking forward to it.'

'Yes, of course,' Pollard muttered. 'Quite understandable.'

'How long have you been out here, Pollard?' Garrett asked, putting his coffee cup down.

'In Ireland? Three years, sir. Stormont first. Then a year as an agent in the field. I was posted to Newry last April.'

'What sort of facilities do you have?'

'The department — I use the word very loosely — consists of myself, an admin assistant and a part-time secretary. We've got mainframe access, direct nonintervention phone lines to Stormont, the standard electronic gear.'

'What's your personal security clearance rating?'

'B-4, sir.' Garrett nodded. Pollard's place in the scheme of things was that of a branch manager in a very large conglomerate. The nature of what he did and where he did it made it inevitable that he would have a low ranking on the need-to-know scale. Clearances were rated upwards from C to A, in three to six character codings:

C-1, the lowest grade, permitted access only to material with single-character codings, usually 'soft' intelligence. 'Hard', or top-secret intelligence was rarely rated much lower than A-3. Pollard would have access to only medium-grade intelligence material.

Garrett took out his ID and showed it to Pollard.

'A-6,' Pollard said softly.

'Know what that means?'

'Yes, sir. It means you can talk to God on a man-to-man basis.'

'And that's just what I'm going to do, Pollard,' Garrett said. 'But first I want to ask you something. Do you know Stephen Elkins?'

A frown creased the boyish face. 'I think I've met him, sir,' he said. 'He's senior liaison at Stormont, isn't he?'

'How about Major Patterson, head of MI?'

Pollard shook his head. 'Why do you ask?'

'Not important,' Garrett said. 'You've told me what I want to know. That's all. Now, I've got some telephoning to do.'

★　★　★

As soon as he had the room to himself, Garrett dialled the 071 code for London followed by the treble-four prefix and eight-digit number that would connect him directly with Neal McCaskill, deputy Director of Analysis at the security services computer complex on the twelfth floor of Euston Tower in London. The Marylebone Road building also housed both DI5's operations division and the postal investigations department on the twenty-fifth floor. Not at all coincidentally, both were sandwiched by the records and statistical information divisions of British Telecom and the Department of Social Security.

'Hello.'

No one gave names or numbers at the Glass House. Anyone who got through either had the daily code or the connection was immediately broken.

'Today's clearance is Zodiac,' Garrett said, giving the codeword Pollard had provided. 'This is Charles Garrett, clear-ance UMBRA, code PACT, do you wish me to spell phonetically?'

'Dinna bother, laddie,' a rich Scottish voice replied. 'I recognized your voice right away.'

'Hello, Mac,' Garrett said.

'Where are ye, Garrett?'

'A long way from home, Mac,' Garrett said. 'And I need some help.'

'That's all I ever hear from ye, laddie,' McCaskill said. 'I sometimes wonder how your lot ever function without us poor slaves of the VDU. What is it this time?'

'I need a brute-force search. UMBRA priority.'

'Do ye, now?' McCaskill said. 'And do I just drop all the other priority work that's piled up here to make room for yours, or what?'

'Mac, I can't do it where I am. The local man has only got a B-4 rating. His Cryptag won't access at the level I want.'

He heard the Scotsman's rich chuckle. 'Then you'd appear to be up the proverbial creek, laddie.'

'I can go through Bleke if you want me to.'

'No need for threats,' Mac said, and Garrett could almost see him smiling. McCaskill and Bleke were about as compatible as two fighting bantam cocks.

'I've got three names, Mac. I want profiles. Everything we've got on them, right down to the last time they changed their underwear.'

'Ye'd better give me a location first,' McCaskill told him.

'Newry, Northern Ireland. DI5 Outstation 47.'

'Ye say ye canna access us from there?'

'I can receive, but I can't send or access above B-4.'

'Go back to Belfast. Do it there.'

'Undesirable.'

'Och, wonderful,' McCaskill said disgustedly. 'Aye, well, then ye'll have to play leapfrog, laddie. D'ye ken how?'

'I've done it before,' Garrett said. 'Leapfrog' involved using the huge R2 computer in London to locate a computer it could talk to, and which could, in turn, talk to the one Garrett was using. 'The access code for this office is D-Donald, I-Iceberg, five hypen one eight four eight

277

seven seven three seven double-X.'

'Got it,' McCaskill said. 'And the names?'

'Michael Conlan. C-Charlie — '

'Och, dinna bother wi' all that phonetics shit, Charles, there's naught wrong with my ears,' McCaskill rasped. 'Michael Conlan, with an 'a'?'

'Right. James Bounden, with an 'e'. And Peter Nash.'

'What do you want?'

'Everything we've got. Anything TREVI might have. I want each name trawled five ways. Once for the name Daniel Flynn, that's with two 'n's. Once each for common denominators of time, place, and background. And once each against the name Sean Hennessy. That's — '

'I know that one, laddie,' McCaskill said.

'Thought you might,' Garrett told him. 'I can quote you the file reference by heart. PACT-three eight two four nine two nine eight, stroke H. For Hennessy.'

'Well,' McCaskill said softly. 'Sean Hennessy, eh? I think I could safely say I'll be able to persuade the boys to try really hard on this one. Stand by at your end. When it comes through it will come in a ruddy blush.'

'Go to it, Mac,' Garrett said, and hung up.

McCaskill was as good as his word. Within an hour, the telephone rang again. It was Henry Fryer, McCaskill's chief of operations.

'I think we've got what you want, sir,' he said. 'How do you want it, onscreen or hard copy?'

'Onscreen,' Garrett said. 'Do not, repeat do not, print.'

'Affirmative,' Fryer said. 'Stand by.'

Garrett watched the screen. It blinked, darkened momentarily, then a cursor appeared, with a tiny bleep.

* * *

READY FOR TRANSMISSION: KEY CODING CLEARANCE NOW. Garrett typed in his code clearance and waited. CLEARANCE SANCTIONED: KEY PERSONAL CLEARANCES NOW. He keyed in his secret personal code and the

279

machine blinked again, once, twice, and then lines of information zipped across the screen almost too fast for the eye to follow.

CLASSIFICATION UMBRA RED
YOUR EYES ONLY
CORRUPT AFTER READING

BOUNDEN, JAMES JOHN: for complete dossier key
JJB-W67120Z
CONLAN, MICHAEL: for complete dossier key
MC-D58329K
NASH, PETER GEORGE: for complete dossier key
PGN-CRMG-93462P

Trawlsearch results:

#1 Common denominator: Sean Hennessy
Results: key SHD — 1
#2 Common denominator: Daniel Flynn
Results: key DF — 2
#3 Common denominator: place/time/

How the hell did we ever get along before they invented computers? he wondered. He typed in the first coding and watched as the information flooded the screen. Two hours later, he had everything he needed to know. Michael Conlan had not only gone to the same Dungannon grammar school, but also been a member of the East Tyrone brigade of the IRA at the same time as Hennessy. Bounden and Nash had also been members of the same unit later, in the early seventies; natural candidates for any unit that Hennessy might put together.

Bounden was among those listed as suspects in the IRA bombings of British Army barracks at Mill Hill in August 1988, and near Market Drayton, Shropshire, the following February. Nash was believed to have been one of the occupants of a flat in Clapham who fled abandoning one hundred and fifty pounds of Semtex just before the place was raided by Scotland Yard's antiterrorist arm SO13; it was suspected he might also have been the killer of a would-be car thief who was shot trying to break into a Renault parked outside the flat. All this linked them very firmly with Hennessy, who had been the leader of a bomb squad hitting military targets in northern Germany, and who was believed to have found refuge in the UK after his unit was neutralized.

It was when he came to the trawl on Danny Flynn that Garrett got the biggest surprises. For the past three or four years, Danny had been playing a dangerous double game: acting on the one hand as a spotter — someone who identified, located and set up for assassination IRA informers and sympathizers — for the Ulster Defence Association, a violent paramilitary loyalist organization. At the same time he had been spying on the UDA and passing the information to Eamonn Nash, brother of Peter Nash, leader of an IRA punishment squad rated Most Sought by the RUC and high on the British security services' AAC — apprehend at any cost — list. The link explained how Danny had been able to come up with hard information on

Hennessy. And also why he had been killed: his cover had been blown somehow — or by someone. The men of violence showed no mercy to anyone who doublecrossed them.

The R2 trawl of common denominators — comparing the movements of each of the named men on a time, place and background basis — provided a massive series of possible leads, but Garrett was in no longer in the mood to play detective and did not allow himself to be distracted by them. He used the computer search facility to refine again and again the information from CSR — casual surveillance reports — which the R2 mainframe in London had disgorged until, at last, the machine came up with what he had been looking for. He leaned back in the chair, smiling at the lines on the computer screen.

>>>>>BOUNDEN, JAMES

14 June 1989. CSR-DI5: Bryansford with Nash
18 June 1989. CSR-DI6: Castlewellan with Conlan

21 June 1989. CSR-UDR: Dundrum with Conlan

28 June 1989. CSR-UDR: Maghera

>>>>>CONLAN, MICHAEL

12 June 1989. CSR-UDR: Bryansford

16 June 1989. CSR-UDR: Castlewellan

21 June 1989. CSR-DI5: Dundrum with Bounden

25 June 1989. CSR-RUC: Newcastle

>>>>>NASH, PETER

14 June 1989. CSR-DI5: Bryansford with Bounden

23 June 1989. CSR-UDR: Newcastle with Conlan

26 June 1989. CSR-RUC: Dundrum

>>>>>LIST ALL KNOWN IRA SAFE HOUSES INSIDE AREA BOUNDED BY: BRYANSFORD, CASTLEWELLAN, DUNDRUM, MAGHERA AND NEWCASTLE,

COUNTY DOWN, NI
>>>>ONLY ONE FOUND:
Wateresk Hill Farm, ½ km north of
B180 Dundrum — Maghera road

'Got you, you sonofabitch,' Garrett said.

17

After carefully briefing Pollard on his role in the scenario that was about to unfold, Garrett signed out a pair of French-made OB-42 passive binoculars, twenty-eight rounds of Equaloy 9 mm ammunition, and a trio of what were known in the service as 'fireworks' — Mark III standard CS gas grenades made by a Wiltshire firm famous for more user-friendly products — and spent perhaps fifteen minutes picking out one or two more exotic items. That done, he selected the clothing and supplies he knew he would need: heavy woollen sweaters, Barbour waterproofs, stout Timberland walking boots with cleated soles, body warmers, thermal underwear.

It was almost two in the afternoon when Garrett crossed the bridge over the Carrigs River and turned right by the pub at the T-junction in the centre of Maghera. Huge dark clouds loomed over the mountains behind him; rain lashed down, drumming on the roof of the car. A long flat line of light lay along the horizon to the east; the sea was no longer visible. The road ran almost due east alongside Wateresk Hill, past a sewage works sited on the riverside, then forked left toward Dundrum. He saw a signpost for Moneylane and Magherasaul; he turned left, and after travelling perhaps five hundred yards, left again into a single-track lane going uphill. He hoped no halfdrowned farmer, heading home in his tractor with his head down, was coming the other way: visibility was almost zero.

A rickety-looking wooden sign by the roadside pointed to Wateresk Hill Farm. He could see the grey stone buildings huddled together at the end of a narrow muddy track scoured into the stony earth along the swell of the hill, about two hundred and fifty feet above sea level, he reckoned. He took his binoculars out of the glove compartment. Nothing moved on the drowning land. A long wooden barn and hayloft abutted an L-shaped milking shed, and another long low building that looked like a dairy formed the third side of an incomplete rectangle surrounding a huge square water trough with an iron pump at its centre. Behind and to one side of the cattle shed was the stone farmhouse, yellow light spilling from mullioned windows.

Not too bad, he thought; but not wonderful, either. There was cover he could use, of course: a copse of trees here, a cattle trough there, hedgerows, manure piles; but the farmhouse itself would be difficult for any group of men to get near without being seen. He made a threepoint turn then drove back the way he had come. About halfway, he stopped the car and got out in the slanting rain, lifting one of the small waterproof duffel bags he had packed earlier from the back seat. He trudged across the fields to a copse of trees and stashed the duffel bag and another, smaller plastic sack into a shelving declivity beneath one of the larger trees.

Wet and cold in spite of the protective clothing, he slopped his way back to the car and got in. He put the heater on full and turned on the fan; the windows steamed up anyway. He followed the lane to the main road and drove on from there to Dundrum. The old Norman round keep on its wooded hill above the town looked cheerless against the puce sky.

He found a café in a side street, a small, yellow-painted place about fifty feet long and ten wide, with Formica-topped tables fixed end-on to the walls. The man behind the glass-fronted counter near the door was big and burly, and his greying hair was close cropped. His wife, also burly but determinedly blonde, did the cooking in a small kitchen, passing the food through a hatchway to the man.

'Ask you a question?' he said to the owner.

'What'd that be?' the man said, his accent pure Ards.

'Is there a florist anywhere nearby?'

The man frowned. 'Florist? Aye, there's Docherty's at the end of Main Street. You'll see the sign.'

The place was easy to find; a neat white Vauxhall Astra van was parked outside with a painted legend that said 'E.

Docherty — Flowers for all Occasions. Wreaths and Wedding Bouquets a Speciality'. The young fellow sitting in the cubbyhole at the rear of the shop that served as an office was twenty-two at the most. A mug of tea steamed on the desk in front of him.

'Flowers,' Garrett said. 'I want to send some.'

'Ar,' the youth said, getting to his feet. He went to the rear door. 'Eileen!' he yelled. 'Shop!' He came back and sat down again. 'I only do deliveries, see,' he explained. After a moment or two, a young woman in a heavy wool sweater and dark blue jeans came in carrying a bundle of greenery. She had a mop of naturally curly dark hair and the bright mischievous blue eyes of a schoolgirl.

'Sorry to keep you waiting,' she said, in a breathy little-girl voice. 'Sure I wasn't expecting much custom on such a day as this.'

'I'd like to order a bouquet,' Garrett told her. 'For delivery tomorrow.'

'How much did you want to spend?'

'Oh, about ten pounds.'

That cheered her up. 'Local, is it?'

'Moneylane way,' he said.

'That shouldn't be any problem,' she said with a smile. 'We've not a lot on tomorrow.'

'It's most important that the flowers are delivered between two and two-thirty,' Garrett said. 'Can you manage that?'

'Kevin?'

Young Acne looked up blankly. 'Aye, what?'

'Look in the book and see what we've got between two and three tomorrow.'

He picked up a cheap duplicate book and leafed through it. He shook his head. 'Nothing tomorrow.'

'That'll be fine, then,' Eileen said briskly. He gave her the name, Bridget Riley, told her the address, and paid for the flowers and delivery.

'What about a card?' she asked.

Garrett shook his head. 'They're a surprise,' he said. 'Don't let me down now, will you, Kevin?'

'No way, José,' Kevin told him.

Garrett went back to the car and drove up Main Street towards the seafront, turning south on to the A2. The road bent round the windwhipped waters of Dundrum Inner Bay. Garrett drove well inside the speed limit, making a mental map of the area as he passed through it, noting the location of car parks, bridges, caravan sites and small factory buildings along his route. The rain was still coming down, cold grey lines drawn against a darker grey sky, lashing the fairways of the Royal County Down Golf Club on the rolling dunes between the road and the sea. When he got to Newcastle, the streets of the little seaside town were as empty as if it had been neutron-bombed. The sweeping three-mile crescent of beach looked wild and bleak, the Mourne mountains beyond shrouded in grey cloud and drifting mist.

He pulled into the car park of the Slieve Donard Hotel on Downs Road. The place was deserted, Muzak the only sound in the carpeted foyer. He pressed the button on the desk and after a few moments a young woman came out of a back room, smiling at something someone inside had said.

'Can I help you?'

She was small and plump, dressed in a black suit and a white blouse with a frilly front. Her hair was red-gold and she had a cute, insouciant mouth. The plastic badge on her left lapel announced that her name was Sian.

'I'd like a room . . . Sian, is it?'

'How long would you be staying, sir?'

'Just the night,' Garrett said.

'Yes, sir,' she said. 'Sign in, please?'

If she noticed his soaked trenchcoat or his mudstained shoes and clothing, her expressionless face betrayed no interest. He was just a chore she had to do before she went back to whatever had sent her smiling from the room in the back. Garrett signed the book and scribbled his signature on the credit-card blank the girl put in front of him. A youngster in an ill-fitting black suit showed him to a clean, functional room on the second floor that looked out over the garden to the mountains beyond. Gusts of wind rattled rain against the windows.

'Nice day,' Garrett said.

'Aye,' the youth said. 'Murder.' He

looked as if he ought to be in school memorizing Archimedes' Principle.

'The girl at reception. Sian? What's her other name?'

'Riley, sir.'

'Local girl?'

'Aye,' the lad said. 'She comes from over Maghera.'

By the time the young porter left with his pound tip, Garrett had confirmed that John Riley was still the owner of Wateresk Hill Farm and ran the place alone with his wife Bridget. According to the young porter, Sian's brothers Anthony and Patrick were welders at the shipyards in Belfast. Thanks to R2 in London, Garrett already knew that John Henry Riley, forty-eight, came from Valentia Island in Dingle Bay. His wife, Bridget, forty-four, was a local girl who had married Riley in 1965 at the pretty nineteenth-century parish church in Castlewellan. The girl's family had been dairy farmers at Wateresk for three generations. Bridget's father had been a militant Republican who had early pledged his support to Sinn Fein and the army, and brought his family up to do likewise. Anyone who married into it adopted the same stance. Although John Riley had never borne arms or planted bombs, his door was always open to the men who did.

Garrett got out of his muddy clothes and changed into trousers and a sweat-shirt. He went down to the pool and swam a lazy twenty lengths, then languished for perhaps half an hour in the sauna to get the damp ache out of his bones. Later still, he had some food sent up to his room; when he had finished eating, he called London.

'I been cheated, been mistreated, when will I be loved?' he said, when Jessica answered the phone.

'Before I answer, is that Don or Phil?'

'That's what I like about you. So unattainable.'

'Where are you?' she said.

'Where the mountains o' Mourne sweep down to the sea,' he told her.

'Oh, how lovely! I've always wanted to go there.'

'You wouldn't care for it right now. It's blowing a gale and it's very, very wet.'

'Well, it's autumn.'

'In Northern Ireland it's always autumn,' Garrett said. 'Tell me what you've been doing.'

'You know what an exciting life I lead. Mending broken psyches, patching up burned-out cases. How about you?'

'I won't bore you. Let me ask you a question instead.'

'Ah, the ulterior motive emerges,' Jessica said. 'And I thought you'd called just so you could fantasize about my fair white body.'

'I do that all the time,' Garrett grinned. 'Here's the problem. I've got two outsize egos. They hate each other. One of them hates women, the other can't get enough. Your starter for ten is, which of them works for the IRA?'

'Is this a serious question?'

'I know you're a genius, Dr Goldman, but even you can't come up with a diagnosis on the basis of that much information.'

'Wrong,' Jessica said. 'You're describing a fairly classic syndrome. Management psychologists run up against it all the time. It could well be that these two men have set themselves up in adversarial rôles because each detects in the other things he hates, either about life generally or about himself in particular. Well, perhaps not hates: dislikes, disapproves of. They assume rôles not unlike a husband and wife in an unhappy marriage. They play the same games: Now Look What You Made Me Do, Why Should I Change When It's You That's Wrong, I Wouldn't Have This Problem If It Wasn't For You, I Knew You'd Say That, You Don't Love Me Any More, all the cliché marital ploys writ large. But that doesn't mean I can answer your question.'

'I never really thought you could,' Garrett said. 'I just wanted to hear your voice.'

'You sound down.'

'I'll be all right. Tough day ahead, that's all.'

'I wish I were there.'

'Not as much as I do. Goodnight, Jess. I love you.'

'I love you, too. Come home to me soon.'

He looked at his watch. Ten o'clock. He would have enjoyed a drink, but discarded the notion. He turned out the lights and got into bed. After what seemed like a long, long time, he slept.

★   ★   ★

He awoke, shivering.

The rain had stopped. He pulled back the curtains and looked out at the first light in the predawn sky. Time to go. He put on the survival clothes he had brought with him from Newry, packing his other stuff into a duffel bag to go into the boot of the car. He loaded the ASP Smith & Wesson with the deadly Equaloy rounds, nylon-coated lightweight aluminum bullets which travelled three times faster, and delivered on-target impact ten times greater, than conventional lead bullets. He stowed everything else he would need in the pockets of the all-weather clothing, and went silently on his way.

First light was reflecting on the shifting surface of the dark grey sea as he parked the car above the beach and set off on foot towards Wateresk Hill Farm. The wind off the water had an edge like a knife and he was grateful for the protective warmth of the Barbour jacket. The ground was soft and spongy with rain, and more than once his feet sank above the ankles in mud. About a quarter of a mile above the Dundrum road the ground rose quite sharply and he was breathing heavily by the time he got within sight of the farm.

Looking more or less north up the hill, he could see a low privet hedge, an angle-iron swing with a wooden seat, the kitchen garden sloping up towards the rear of the two-storey stone farmhouse. To the right of it was the long, low single-storey stone building that housed the dairy, with a purpose-built lean-to used for rearing veal calves. Beyond it, on the north side of the farmyard, were the L-shaped milking barn and cattle byres. Still further on was a closed barn that was used to keep the tractors and farm machinery in.

No lights showed anywhere. Off to the

far right-hand side of the yard, sheltered by four sturdy oaks, was the hayloft with a curved roof of corrugated iron which was Garrett's destination. He eased through the hedge, ignoring the sharp pull of the brambles, using the thick trunks of the oak trees as a screen. The hayloft was about three-quarters full, the cubes of dried hay stacked all the way up to the roof in steps and stairs like a child's blocks. Once at the top, Garrett made a square of hay bales in which he could sit comfortably. Behind the house a rooster crowed, another challenged. He set the surveillance glasses on the bale in front of him and sat back to wait.

He did not have to wait long. At about five-thirty, lights went on in an upstairs room in the farmhouse. A little after six, a short, sturdy figure came out of the door, followed by a black Labrador bitch and a black and white Border collie. The man was of medium height, with sloping, powerful shoulders. He wore a heavy leather waistcoat over a thick sweater, dark cords tucked into rubber boots, and a flat cap. Garrett watched him through the glasses; it was John Riley. He crossed the yard, opening up the heavy wooden double doors of the milking parlour, then went through the gate and disappeared from Garrett's field of vision up the track leading to the road.

Lights spilled out of the downstairs windows of the farmhouse. A buxom woman in dark clothing came out of the back door carrying a plastic bowl. Bridget Riley, on her way to let out the chickens and gather the day's egg yield for breakfast. The thought of fresh eggs and bacon made his stomach rumble. The gentle lowing of cattle drifted down the hill; a big black and white Friesian lumbered into view, her udders swollen. Others followed. One or two of them went to the big trough in the centre of the yard. The dogs ran between them, tongues hanging out. John Riley came down the path, ho-hoing the laggards along. Bridget Riley came into the yard and flapped her arms at the cows. They swung their heads uncertainly. A mud-spattered Jersey led the way into the milking parlour. One by one the others followed, feet clattering on the stone, evacuating as they went. After a while Garrett could hear the hum of the milking machine.

Riley smoked a cigarette outside, then went into the milking parlour. After a while, a cow lurched out into the yard, followed by another and then two more. When they were all out, Riley and the two dogs herded them on their way back up the hill to the pasture; when they were all through the gate, he shut it and called the dogs back. Then he went back into the milking parlour to help his wife clean it out. It was about an hour and a half before he came out again, looked about, scratched his crotch. He said something over his shoulder and Bridget Riley emerged, wiping her hands on her apron. She went back to the house. Riley sat on the edge of the cattle trough and smoked another cigarette. When he was finished, he tossed the butt aside and stood up.

'Tess! Barney! Breakfast!'

The dogs were smart; they knew the word and raced ahead of their master to the house, standing on hind legs and pawing at the door. Garrett checked his watch: eight o'clock. After breakfast would come the chore of cleaning up the yard, then feeding the livestock. There was never any shortage of work on a farm. He snatched up the glasses as the back door opened and Bridget Riley came out with a tray covered by a white cloth. She came along the path between the end of the milking sheds and the dairy building, and opened a stable-type door facing the yard. When she came out she had no tray. It was starting to rain; she padlocked the door and ran for the house.

Garrett slid down from his eyrie and eased round behind the dairy building, past the heated stalls in which the young calves being reared for veal were kept. The long single-storey stone building was divided into four sections: at the end nearest the house was the tiled and stone floored dairy with its pasteurizing machinery; the other three were one-time stables, now used to store various kinds of farm tools and equipment, ranging from scythes to harrows. He squinted in through the cobwebbed window at the

303

rear of the old stable which Bridget Riley had gone into. Sitting on a bale of straw with an old horse blanket over her shoulders, both hands around a steaming mug of tea, was Patricia Burke.

He made no sound; all he needed to know was where she was. If she knew he was nearby, she might well betray that knowledge to one of her captors and precipitate disaster. Male voices approaching made him freeze against the rear wall of the dairy. John Riley was coming out of the house with two other men, all of them wearing yellow rubberized coats of the type worn by motorway maintenance workers. Two of the men went into the storehouse and got out stiff brooms; the third — Garrett confirmed it was Riley with a quick glance around the corner of the building — turned on the powerful hosepipe and played it on the cow manure splattered around the yard. The two men with the brooms worked ahead of the water, brushing the manure into a single pile. Now he could see them. One of them was Michael Conlan. The other was Sean Hennessy.

Garrett's hand touched the butt of the ASP Smith & Wesson. He shook his head. This was no time for impulsive action. He didn't even know for sure how many men Hennessy had with him; Walton, the Craigthomas administrator, had said there were six of them. Placing his feet with infinite care, he eased back along the rear wall of the outbuilding, heading back to the concealment of the hayloft. There he settled behind the French surveillance binoculars and watched and waited.

A little while after they finished sweeping the yard, a red Post Office van came bumping down the track. Hennessy and Conlan saw it coming and disappeared into the house. The young postman got out of his van, gave Riley some letters and a small packet, and stood for a few minutes talking before going on his way. Riley took the post inside. At about eleven-thirty he came out again and went around back to the covered barn. Garrett heard the roar of a tractor starting up. A few minutes later, Riley reappeared, towing a heavy trailer behind the Massey-Ferguson, which he stopped outside the storehouse. The sound of his shouts was swamped by the heavy engine. He threw open the wooden doors and started heaving bales of hay on to the trailer. Four men came out of the house and across the yard to help him. Garrett zoomed in on their faces: the only one he recognized was the slender, blond Jim Bounden.

That made six of them altogether.

Riley shouted something over the roar of the tractor engine and the four men jumped up on the trailer, hanging on as Riley wheeled the machine around the yard and bumped up the stony track towards the upper pasture. A movement at the rear of the house caught Garrett's eye. Bridget Riley had come out of the house and was pulling up a cabbage from the kitchen garden. As she did, Sean Hennessy came to the door, a mug in his hand. He leaned against the door jamb and said something to Bridget Riley. She made as if to slap him, and he ducked, grinning widely. The door closed.

Time passed; the rain thinned, died. Garrett sucked glucose tablets and waited. The roar of the tractor approaching prompted him to check his watch. Nearly one o'clock. The old man was coming home for his lunch. The big Massey-Ferguson wheeled into the yard and Riley brought it to an abrupt stop beside the cattle trough. The four men who had gone with him to feed the live stock jumped off.

'Going to rain again, Johnnie?' one of them shouted.

'Piss down,' Riley replied, switching off the engine. 'Like as not.'

'Better get inside,' said one of the others. 'What's Bridget got for dinner?'

'Irish stew . . . '

' . . . in the name of the law!'

They went into the house, laughing at their own schoolboy humour. After ten minutes, Bridget Riley came out bearing a tray, which was covered as before with some kind of cotton dishcloth. She went to the door she had opened earlier and walked in. Then she emerged, turned the key in the padlock and hurried back to the house, carrying the tray she had brought Patricia Burke's breakfast on.

When the farmhouse door closed behind her, Garrett slid down from the hayloft again and made his way around in back of the dairy. On his earlier foray he had seen a solid steel crowbar leaning against the wall. He took it back to the far end of the building and came round the front from the far end, making it almost impossible for anyone in the house to see him. He jammed the crowbar into the hasp of the padlock and put some torque on it. The metal hasp made a spanging sound and burst open.

'You!' Patricia Burke gasped. 'How did you — '

'Never mind all that,' Garrett told her urgently. He handed her the small duffel bag he had brought with him. It contained thermal underwear, waterproof trousers and jacket, a Viyella man's shirt and a heavy wool sweater. 'As soon as I've gone, get into these clothes. There are three pairs of boots. One ought to fit you; if they're a fraction too big, use two pairs of socks. Have you got a watch?'

She shook her head. 'They took it away.'

'Count elephants,' he said. 'When you get around the eighteen hundred mark, stand by to make a run for it. All right?'

'Yes,' she said, breathing rapidly. 'Yes, all right.'

'Good girl.' He squeezed her arm and went out, closing the door and pushing the broken padlock together so that it looked intact. He reeled back along the front of the building to the hayloft and looked up the hill towards the gateway at the end of the rutted track.

'Come on, Kevin,' he muttered. 'Get your arse in gear.'

18

A little after two-fifteen, the white van with the legend 'E. Docherty — Flowers for all Occasions' turned into the track leading down to the farm. From behind the hayloft, Garrett watched it through the binoculars. Young Acne was smack on time and he was alone. The van bumped to a stop in the farmyard. Kevin got out and walked round to the farmhouse door, whistling. Bridget Riley answered his knock, a frown on her face.

'Good day to yez,' Kevin said cheerfully. 'Mrs Riley, is it?'

'Aye,' she said warily. 'What do you want?'

Kevin handed her the bouquet, prettily wrapped in a clear plastic protective bag, a bow of pink ribbon around the base. He held out his clipboard and pen.

'If you'll just sign here,' he said.

'There must be some mistake,' the puzzled woman told him. 'Who are these from?'

'No idea, missis,' Kevin said cheerfully. 'Big fellow came into the shop yesterday and ordered them. Asked special for them to be delivered between two and two-thirty. Good, eh?'

He grinned, expecting praise.

'You'd better be after takin' them back where you brought them from,' Bridget Riley told him angrily. 'There's no one expecting flowers here.'

'You're Mrs Riley, Wateresk Hill Farm?'

'Of course I am, you stupid bugger!' she snapped.

'Well, I don't under — ' Kevin's voice trailed off. Sean Hennessy had appeared in the stone hallway behind Bridget Riley and was looking at him over the barrel of a levelled Armalite rifle.

'In here!' Hennessy rasped. 'On the floor. Flat!'

'Jesus, mister!' Kevin managed, his voice half an octave higher. Rough hands thrust him to the ground and frisked him.

'He's clean,' someone said. He looked up. There were half a dozen men in the hallway. Some of them had handguns. O Jesus, he thought, O sweet Mary mother of God, don't let them kill me.

'Get on your feet, you little turd!' Hennessy barked at the prostrate delivery boy. Kevin scrambled to get up. He was literally shaking with terror.

'Who sent you here?' Hennessy demanded. 'Who sent you?'

Kevin shook his head. His mouth was bone-dry, his tongue stuck to the roof of his mouth. Hennessy slapped him across the face, right, left. Tears sprang to Kevin's eyes. He stared helplessly at the angry faces ringing him.

'I never . . . I just . . . deliver,' he managed, shaking his head from side to side to show them he had nothing to do with whatever it was they wanted to know.

'Who sent you?' Hennessy shouted at him. 'Who sent these fucking flowers?'

'Don't know, mister!' Kevin gasped. 'This man.'

'What man, damn you?' Hennessy grabbed hold of Kevin's blue denim overall and shook him so that his head snapped back and forward and his teeth clattered. 'What man?'

'I never looked,' Kevin whined. 'I only deliver, see?'

'Let go of the lad, Sean,' Michael Conlan said. 'Can't you see he's scared shitless? Now, lad, tell me this: did you by any chance see the man?'

The gentle voice gave Kevin hope. He turned pleadingly towards the speaker. 'Big fellow, he was,' he said eagerly. 'English. Powerful built. Hard-looking man.'

'Jesus Christ!' Hennessy said, thrusting the delivery boy aside. He ran out of the house and across to the stone building where Patricia Burke had been held. The others ran out after him, leaving Kevin gawking in the hallway. The stable door was banging in the wind. Patricia Burke was gone.

★   ★   ★

As Kevin got out of the van with the flowers, Garrett slipped along the front of the dairy building, the ASP Smith & Wesson in his right hand. He knocked the broken padlock off its hasp and opened the stable door. Patricia Burke was standing inside, her face and body tight with tension.

'Come on!' Garrett snapped, holding out a hand. She was wearing the clothes he had brought her; the weather-proofs were a size too large, giving her a little-girl-lost look, but at least they were warm. There was colour in her cheeks again. She ran lightly alongside Garrett, who led the way through an iron gate between the dairy building and the hayloft, and along the far side of the hedge running down the slight slope toward the Dundrum road about six hundred yards away. Halfway down the hill was the stand of trees where Garrett had stashed the duffel bags earlier. They reached it without incident and slid to a stop, panting. Their boots and leggings were already coated with mud.

'So far, so good,' Garrett said.

As he spoke, he felt heavy drops of rain on his face. Thanks a lot, he thought, looking at the sky. He stretched prone behind one of the trees, watching the farm through the binoculars. The delivery boy had gone inside. It wouldn't be long.

'How are the boots?' he asked her.

'I take size six. These are fine.'

'Just in case something happens to me' he said. 'I want you to take this.'

He gave her the Heckler & Koch HK4 self-loading pistol that he had wrapped in the smaller plastic bag. It was the eight-shot .32 calibre model and weighed less than a pound unloaded. She stared at it and then at him.

'I can't,' she said.

'Take it,' he told her. 'Put it in your pocket.'

She started to protest but he held up a hand, scanning the farmhouse through his binoculars. He saw Hennessy run out of the house and disappear behind the dairy building. It had hit the fan.

'Come on!' he said to Patricia Burke, and led the way at a steady lope across the open fields towards the road below. The speckle of rain he had felt earlier now turned into a downpour. He thought he heard the sound of a car or lorry engine but he could not be sure; the wind was getting stronger, too. Faint shouts came from behind them up the hill. He stopped and turned. Four figures were coming down after them, spread across the slope in a straggling line.

'Get down to the hedge at the bottom and wait for me!' Garrett shouted to Patricia Burke, who lifted a hand to show that she had heard then ran, lurching on the treacherously soft ground, towards the road. Garrett waited until the four men were about a hundred yards away then knelt and levelled the ASP at the nearest of them, a short, slope-shouldered figure in a dark blue pea jacket. He fired three spaced shots and thought the man faltered. There were shouts of alarm and the quartet dropped flat in the soaking mud. Garrett heard the flat blap of small-arms fire, but the rain drowned any sound the slugs might have made if they came near him.

Patricia Burke was waiting by the hedge, back turned to the rain. He gave her a boost over and she slid down into the ditch bordering the road. He forced his own way through after her and slid down beside her, pointing across the road.

'Car,' he panted. 'Car park. By the beach.'

She nodded and ran across the road, climbing an iron gate on the far side that led into the marshy triangle of fields formed by the Maghera-Dundrum road, the narrower lane that branched off it towards Slidderyford Bridge, and the old coast road, superseded long since by the new A2 that paralleled it. Three of the four men were running down the hill fast now, weaving and dodging. The fourth was sitting in the mud, out of it. Garrett waited until they were perhaps fifty yards away then ran flat out across the road and vaulted over the gate.

As soon as he was on the far side, he lobbed all three of the CS grenades across the road and to his left, into the wind. They detonated with hard, coughing bangs, and large, dense clouds of CS smoke burst outwards and up, blanketing both sides of the hedge. Without waiting to gauge the effect, Garrett ran for the beach road as fast as the ground would permit, concentrating on keeping his footing on the soft, muddy earth. Patricia Burke was perhaps forty yards in front of him, not running now but moving as fast as she could, her arms flailing to maintain balance.

Garrett caught up with her as they reached the road, and they stopped, heaving for breath, steam coming off them like run horses in the slanting rain. He looked back across the field behind them. A man was climbing over the gate; another followed, then another. Somewhere above them in the murk he heard the heavy muttering whicker of a helicopter. John Pollard was moving in.

'Come on,' Garrett gritted, taking Patricia's hand. They ran across the glistening width of the Newcastle road towards the car park with its forlorn and wind-ripped picnic area. Garrett bundled Patricia into the rear seat and started the car.

'Belt up!' he yelled. 'It's going to get hairy!'

Immediately, a man appeared on the far side of the main road, then another.

Both of them had automatic rifles cradled across their bodies. They saw the smoke pluming from the exhaust of the Sierra and ran towards the car. Garrett gave it the gun.

They were good. One stepped to the right, the other to the left, and both laid accurate automatic fire on the approaching vehicle, the hail of bullets spanging off the windscreen and bodywork. Garrett hit the man on the right as he wheeled the car out on to the road, hurling him in a broken heap against one of the picnic tables. The other emptied his magazine as Garrett made it to the road, but the fusillade had no effect on the specially reinforced bodywork. Then they were away, thundering down the straight, empty road.

★ ★ ★

From the time Hennessy discovered Garrett was gone until the big man's car skidded out of the car park on the beach facing the bay, perhaps not more than ten or twelve minutes had elapsed. In that time, Hennessy had commandeered Johnnie Riley's battered old Land Rover and thrown it at full speed down the long straight lane that led to the Dundrum road, horn blaring as he skidded out of the junction and thundered along the old beach road parallel to the A2, intending to cut the fugitives off. As it was, he got there just as Garrett's car hit Johnny Penketh, smacking him sideways like a scarecrow hit by a hurricane.

Without conscious thought, Hennessy floored the accelerator, racing for the Slidderyford Bridge, where the minor road he was on joined the main A2. He got to it at almost exactly the same moment as Garrett, and powered the big, mud-spattered vehicle out across the road alongside the speeding saloon, striking sparks from its bodywork as the two vehicles smashed into each other. It sounded as if the car had been struck by a mighty hammer.

Garrett fought the wheel as the car's offside tyres left the road, but the vehicle was out of control. Hennessy's Land Rover skidded to a stop, swerving to block the left-hand side of the road as the car swung tail-out, slewing sideways. Garrett heard Patricia scream behind him as the wheels crashed back down, failing to grip at first in the bucketing rain, then gaining traction: he slammed the car into low gear and jammed his foot down, hitting a concrete ramp beside the road that lifted the car four feet into the air and bellyflopping down into a semicircular caravan site overlooking the sand dunes.

Hurling chunks of muddy sand twenty feet into the air behind them, Garrett wrestled for control as the car banged and leaped on the tufted dunes, slaloming forward in long arcing half-circles as the wheels roared and bit, gripping and missing, on the soft wet sand. Hennessy had jumped out of the slewed Land Rover and was running back through the driving rain towards the caravan site, Michael Conlan pounding ten or twenty feet behind him. A car hissed by, headlights blazing, horn blaring at the madmen running along the centre of the main road.

They were about ten yards away when Garrett finally managed to get the car lined up on firm ground and went flat out for the exit of the caravan site, sideswiping an unoccupied caravan as he swung the wheel to hit the road at an angle, relief surging through him as the tyres spun and then bit on the metalled surface and they roared back up towards Slidderyford Bridge. In the driving mirror he saw Hennessy and Conlan running back to the Land Rover, and then he turned left and was round the corner. The car roared over the bridge and he turned left again into the lane that curved around the earthen hump of a chambered grave and an eight-foot-high prehistoric dolmen a few hundred yards further on.

As they surged on to the main road and into Maghera, Garrett checked on his passenger, still seat-belted in the back seat. Patricia Burke's face was paper-white, and she had a trickle of blood on her chin where she had bitten her lip.

'All right?' he said.

'Wonderful,' she replied.

He grinned and passed the car phone

back to her. 'Dial treble four and four eights,' he said. 'Ask to be patched through to John Pollard.'

As she dialled, he swung the car left over Maghera Bridge and pointed it southwest towards Bryansford. Passing the football ground, he saw the Land Rover coming over the bridge behind them, headlights lancing through the grey mist of rain. Long stripes of low cloud that looked like cotton wool streaked the sides of the mountains to their left. Up ahead was the junction with the main road linking Newcastle and Castlewellan. The lights changed from green to red while Garrett was still fifty yards from them. He floored the accelerator and the car surged forward, the Ramjet biting hard and ramming the speedo round to nearly eighty. Garrett took the right-left crossing like a skier in a slalom race, ignoring the blaring horn of a big artic coming down Drumee Hill, easing off the loud pedal as they roared over the slight hump of Bailey's Bridge and into the scatter of houses that was Bryansford.

'I've got Pollard,' Patricia said, her voice tense.

'Tell him Tollymore Park. Tollymore Park.'

He heard her repeat what he had said as the entrance to the nature reserve appeared on the left, and he braked sharply. 'Get ready to bail out,' he shouted, and swung the wheel, skidding slightly on the gravel surface at the entrance to the car park and camping grounds. He threw open the door and grabbed Patricia's hand as she got out, half pulling, half dragging her across the lightly wooded area that led down to the banks of the river running through the reserve. Beyond it, open ground sloped steeply upwards to the lower flanks of Luke's Mountain and Slievenabrock. No sign of the Land Rover. Maybe Hennessy hadn't seen the car turn into the reserve and had overshot, he thought. That would give them a few minutes. They needed them.

'Where are we going?' Patricia shrieked.

'Up into the trees,' he panted. 'Can you make it?'

She nodded vigorously, her wet hair flying. Rain lashed the bare branches of the scattered trees. They ran over the bridge across the Shimna, across the open meadow and around the edge of a small lake from which ducks scattered in quacking panic as they passed. Something whipped through the branches, bringing down a shower of twigs; in the same second, he heard the flat stutter of an automatic weapon. Garrett shoved Patricia down to the ground, diving for shelter from the shooting. He lifted up on his elbows and looked back through the trees. Something moved across the open space below, dark against the darkening greyness. He fired three shots, one to each side and one in the centre of the space where he had seen the movement, aimed to hit about three feet above the ground. The gun was empty; he slid the magazine out of the butt, fed seven bullets into it, and waited.

The woods were silent. There was no bird sound, no insect noise. Nothing moved. The rain continued, steady and hard, driving through the branches of the conifers above them. It was cold.

'What are we going to do?' Patricia hissed. Her dark hair was plastered to her skull and the side of her head. Her face was pinched and her dark eyes looked enormous. He touched her forehead. Her skin was burning.

'We've got to get you somewhere warm,' he said. 'You've got a fever.'

'That damned dairy,' she said, and shivered.

'There's a forestry hut about half a mile away, up there,' he said, gesturing with his chin. 'We'll head for there.'

'What about . . . them?'

'They'll come after us.'

'How do you know?'

'Their retreat is cut off. Hennessy will have checked out my car. He'll know I've whistled up help. He has nowhere left to go. Besides, he's got a score to settle. With both of us.'

'I'm afraid.'

'It's nothing to be ashamed of.'

The wet woods dripped steadily. Still nothing moved. They lay perfectly still, side by side in the hollow between the trees just off the footpath leading steeply up the timber-clad slope. Patricia Burke found herself listening so intently that her jaw ached. She was about to say something when she saw a flicker of movement between the trees off to her left. She touched Garrett's arm. He nodded. He had seen it, too. The steady beat of the rain would have effectively masked the sound of the man's approach. Which of them was it?

The man came out from behind a tree, moving cautiously. He stepped behind another tree trunk, then emerged, quartering across the slope further to their left, obviously trying to work round behind what the pursuers believed to be Garrett's position.

It was Michael Conlan. He wore a thick storm coat, heavy cords and thick-soled rubber boots. The front of his trouser legs were soaked through and his dark hair was plastered to his head as if it had been varnished. In his right hand he carried a .357 Sterling Magnum pistol. He moved again, another tree closer. He ran the back of his left hand across his forehead, wiping water off his eyebrows and cheeks.

Garrett levelled the ASP, waiting. Conlan was maybe fifty feet away, too far for really accurate shooting with a handgun. If he shot and missed, Garrett knew Hennessy would have their position pinpointed. It might well be he had sent Conlan out for just that purpose, and he was somewhere off to the right, a cocked Ingram on his shoulder, ready to rake them with fire the moment he heard the shot.

Conlan flitted between the trees again, nearer now. *Wait*, Garrett told himself. *Wait*. Then all at once Conlan came out of the trees not fifteen feet in front of him. He saw Garrett in the same moment and jerked the big pistol up, firing from the hip like a gunfighter in a western. The boom of the Sterling drowned the lighter crack of the ASP and Garrett heard the heavy slug from Conlan's gun hit a tree trunk a foot away from his head with a stunning thud that made his ears ring.

In front of him Michael Conlan was trying to keep the heavy gun level so that he could fire it again, but the barrel was dropping. He fell to his knees and coughed, and blood came out of his mouth. The dark storm coat was stained by darker blood just above and to the left of the centre of his chest. The big gun fell from his nerveless hand. He looked at Garrett with eyes as blank as copper coins, then pitched forward into the undergrowth.

Garrett was already on the move, rolling away from his former position to a new one behind the thick bole of a huge pine. Patricia Burke looked back over her shoulder at him, her eyes wide, her mouth slightly open in shock or surprise. He made a gesture: this way. He put a finger on his lips. She nodded and moved cautiously towards him, making hardly any sound. Using her heels, she shoved herself along on her back and buttocks until she was behind the tree with Garrett. She was shaking now, and her teeth were chattering. If he didn't get her under cover soon, Garrett thought, she'd get pneumonia.

He stood up carefully, keeping the tree

trunk on the downhill side of his body. He glanced up the hill where the narrow path wound steeply upwards between the dark ranks of the close-serried trees, rising one yard for every two walked.

'Come on,' he said. He took her hand and moved warily through the trees, following the course of a steep-banked stream that chattered its way down the mountainside. He scooped up a handful of water and wet his lips. His mouth was dry with tension. Once, Patricia lost her footing and fell heavily, crying out. Garrett froze, certain that if Hennessy was anywhere nearby, he would have heard the sound. The expected shots did not come. He frowned. Where was he?

Now somewhere off to the north he heard another sound, the flat chattering whistle of helicopter rotors. If he could hear them, Hennessy could hear them too, and would know what it meant. Help was on the way. If he was going to hit, it would have to be soon. He held out his hand and Patricia grabbed it. She did her best to smile, but her mud-streaked face and forlorn appearance negated the effect.

'Chin up,' Garrett said. 'It's not far now.'

The last quarter-mile was a steep scramble that required real effort. Then up ahead of them the path dwindled to nothing, and between the dripping trees they saw the shape of the little forestry cabin with the escarpment of Luke's Mountain steep beyond, and behind it, shrouded in mist, the two-thousand-foot-high massif of Slievenaglogh. They came out of the woods and went round the front of the little hut. The door was ajar and Patricia ran towards it. As Garrett turned to follow her, Sean Hennessy stepped out from the trees skirting the little clearing in front of the hut and shot him through the body.

Garrett was already moving when the bullet hit him, and his own shot tore into Hennessy's body on the right side. The enormous force of the Equaloy bullet hurled him back and down on the ground screaming in agony, his legs kicking high. Garrett staggered against the wall of the forestry hut, his vision misting as the shock of his own wound disorientated him.

He felt someone take hold of him. Patricia Burke put his arm round her shoulder and helped him inside the hut. It was not much bigger than a garden shed, perhaps twelve feet square, with one shuttered window. There was nothing inside except a square wooden table and four bentwood chairs. No one came here except the park rangers and forestry workers. Waves of sickness swept through Garrett's body. He braced himself against the wall to the left of the doorway. He clenched his teeth and forced himself to think clearly. He was hit somewhere low on the left side of the body. How badly didn't matter. Hennessy was still out there. He was down but he wasn't dead.

'Get the gun,' he said to Patricia. 'Dropped my gun.'

She turned towards the door, and as she did, Hennessy kicked it open and staggered in. Garrett's shot had devastated his shoulder and upper right arm. The side of his upper body was a bright red mass of pulsing blood. He held Garrett's ASP at his left side. Garrett looked at him helplessly. Hennessy smiled. His face looked like a skull.

'Remember . . . I told you. Settle it one day, Garrett,' he said. He swayed and steadied himself by bracing his back against the door jamb. His bright blue eyes were unfocused and clouded.

'You're finished, Hennessy,' Garrett said. 'Whatever happens here, you're finished.'

Hatred flooded the Irishman's eyes. He started to laugh, but it turned into a cough. Bright flecks of blood spotted his lips, and Garrett could see the life pulsing out of the man through the devastating wound in his side. There was a total silence all about them. It was as if there was no other world than the one which existed in this tiny wooden cabin, with Hennessy in the doorway, Garrett to his left and Patricia Burke standing with her back to the window opposite them.

'Tell her who you are, Hennessy,' Garrett said.

Hennessy frowned, like a slow learner confronted by a problem from a book he has not yet read. 'What's this, Garrett?' he whispered. 'What fresh perfidy is this?'

Garrett gritted his teeth, willing himself to stay on his feet. Warm blood crept like wet worms down his body. He could feel his head getting light.

'Tell her you're the brave fellow who sent her husband to his death at Portnoo harbour. Tell her it was you who picked him personally to take your place with Paddy McCaffery that day.'

Hennessy lifted the ASP as if it weighed forty pounds. The strength was running out of him like water. His hand was shaking as if with ague. 'You bastard,' he whispered.

'No,' Patricia said. 'Put it down.'

Hennessy turned to face her. She had the deadly looking little HK4 eight-shot automatic Garrett had given her in her hand. Its muzzle was not more than a foot away from Hennessy's forehead. His eyes widened. He let the ASP slip from his fingers; it made a heavy hollow sound as it hit the bare floorboards.

'Don't do this, Patricia,' he said hoarsely. 'Don't betray the man again.'

'You betrayed him,' she said softly. 'You, with your talk of Holy Mother

Ireland, your promises of glory, you with this madness no one can stop. You killed him as surely as if you had done it with your own hands. And now I am going to kill you.'

Desperation seeped into Hennessy's pale blue eyes. 'Wait!' he said hoarsely. 'What about him? Do you know who he is?'

She shook her head. Her eyes were like deep dark holes in the paper whiteness of her face. 'Don't,' she said. 'It's no use.'

' 'twas the British killed Antony Burke,' Hennessy told her. 'Not me, girl. And I'll tell you who sent them soldiers to kill him. That one, there. Charles Garrett.'

'Is it true?' she whispered. Shivers racked her body. Her lips were a bloodless line.

'Yes,' Garrett said.

She looked at him as if she had never seen him before. Then she looked at Hennessy. He nodded, as if confirming what she was thinking. There was a faint smile of triumph on his face. Patricia took a step to one side, the gun moving in an arc between the two of them. Garrett saw what was in Patricia Burke's fever-bright eyes and raised his hand in front of him as if somehow that might stop her.

'Patricia, no!' he said.

'Yes!' she screamed, and fired.

19

'I've got to stop doing this,' Garrett said.

'The doctors said it was touch and go for a while,' Pollard reported. 'But he said you've got an enormous will to live. That's half the battle, it seems.'

'I seem to have been here weeks.'

'This is the third day since . . . Tollymore.'

Garrett rolled his wheelchair over to the window of the conservatory overlooking the garden. It was a clear, bright, sunny morning. He could see people walking on the wide sweep of Newcastle beach.

'How is Patricia?' he asked.

He had passed out a few minutes after she killed Hennessy, and was unconscious when John Pollard arrived with a tough-looking squad of armed uniforms from the RUC Special Support Unit. Ambulances rushed them to a secure private nursing home in Donard Wood, up above the little yacht harbour south of Newcastle Bay.

'They've pumped her full of antibiotics. She just needs rest.'

In his mind's eye he saw the realization dawn on Hennessy's face as Patricia Burke pulled the trigger. The gun bucked in her hand and the bullet hit him just above the right eye and went straight through into the wooden wall. Hennessy collapsed like a marionette whose strings have been cut, his right leg jerking spastically. Patricia Burke's eyes remained fixed on the space where his head had been, staring. Garrett's legs turned to jelly and he slid down the wall into a sitting position.

'Give me the gun,' he said. 'Patricia, give me the gun.'

She bent down and he took the gun out of her hand.

'Tell them I killed him,' he told her urgently. 'Remember. It was me. Remember, Patricia!'

He could feel himself sinking, as if consciousness was above water and he was going under. The last thing he saw as he passed out was Hennessy's dead eyes staring at him.

'You came through like a pro, John,' Garrett told him. 'I'm going to see you get a commendation.'

'It's not over yet,' Pollard said. 'Is it?'

'Not quite,' Garrett replied quietly. 'There are still a couple of loose ends. You handled the whole thing the way I told you?'

Pollard nodded. 'I contacted London. Bleke put a lid on the whole thing. Apart from you, me and Peter Colclough, nobody else knows what happened.'

'Give me a rerun,' Garrett said. 'What happened at Wateresk Hill Farm?'

'We went in at two-thirty precisely, the way you set it up,' Pollard told him. 'Six-man squad, RUC Special Support Group. They found a man called Ronald Williams sitting in the middle of a field with a hole in his thigh the size of a dinner plate. Looked as if someone had shot him with a howitzer. They picked up another man in a car park at the beach: Johnnie Penketh. He wasn't dead, but he had more broken bones than a set of dominoes. Claimed you ran over him in your motor car. Did you?'

'What?' Garrett said, with a grin. 'And risk losing my no claims bonus?'

'The others are all in an RUC max-sec wing at Newry, awaiting disposition,' Pollard said. 'Conlan and Hennessy you know about.'

'If he hadn't been in such a hurry to kill me, he'd probably have done it,' Garrett said. 'He gave me Conlan so he'd have enough time to get up the hill behind us. He had me dead to rights, but he shot too quickly.'

'Pity you couldn't have taken him alive,' Pollard said, almost too casually. There was no hint of a question in the words, but Garrett knew what Pollard was asking him.

'He didn't give me any option, John,' he said. 'I had no choice but to kill him.'

Neither Pollard nor anyone else needed to know what had really happened in the little cabin at the foot of Luke's Mountain. Patricia Burke's epiphany was suffering enough for anyone; he had no intention of letting them subject her to the torture of reliving Hennessy's death.

'All right,' Garrett said. 'You know what happens now.'

'I know. I don't care for it.'

'Nobody cares for treason, John,' Garrett told him. 'Not even the men who commit it.'

Pollard left the room. Garrett stayed by the window for a long time, staring down at the moving, changing changeless sea below. A sailing boat was tacking across the bay and he thought of being on *Sunday Girl* with Diana in the cockpit beside him, her hair blowing in the wind. *He's gone, Diana*, he told her silently. *It's over*.

After a while he wheeled his chair along the corridor to Patricia Burke's room. She was awake, silent, dark eyes staring at the ceiling. She turned her head when he came in, then directed her gaze upward again.

'How are you feeling?'

She swallowed, but made no reply.

'I came to ask your help,' he said. 'Something I need to do.'

Still no reply. He thought he saw tears

shimmering on the edge of shedding. She blinked and they were gone.

'I knew a man,' Garrett said. 'His name was Danny Flynn. Funny little guy, always looked as if he had strayed out of a film made in the fifties. But a very unusual man for all that. He read everything, the classics, thrillers. He knew more about this country's history than a lot of its politicians do.'

'Why are you telling me this?' she whispered, without looking at him.

'Danny . . . got killed. He was working for me. I have to tell his wife. I don't know what to say to her.'

'You think I know?'

'Her name is Moira. She's just a little bit of a thing, like a china doll. She's got four children, another on the way.'

'You die inside,' she said. The answer was unexpected. Garrett said nothing, waiting.

'They tell you, but you don't believe it. Inside you are screaming, it can't be, it can't be! They say all the things people say at times like this. Be strong, they tell you. Life goes on. You'll come through this. But you know you won't. Because you've died, too. Inside.'

She started to cry silently. The tears rolled down the side of her face in streams, soaking the pillow. He sat and watched, not speaking. She wasn't crying for Antony Burke. After a while, she stopped. She got a wodge of Kleenex from the box on the bedside table and dried her eyes.

'I did what you said. I told them you . . . killed him.'

'I know.'

'I keep on seeing it, over and over and over.'

'He would have killed us both, Patricia,' he told her softly. 'Without regret.'

'Regret,' she whispered. 'How odd that you would use that word.'

She turned her head to face him and reached out a hand. He took it in both of his own and held it tight. They sat together like that for quite a long time, no words passing between them. Then she sighed and closed her eyes. He turned the wheelchair round and opened the door.

As he went out she opened her eyes.

'Thank you, Charles,' she said.

★ ★ ★

A little after two, an ambulance took Garrett back to Wateresk Hill Farm. The weather had changed again and sullen clouds coloured the sky with a palette of watery greys. The fountain erected as a memorial to songwriter Percy French slipped past the window. A few hardy souls were playing golf on Murlough Banks. As they passed the caravan site, Garrett allowed himself a small smile: his tyre tracks were still there, scoured into the sand.

John Pollard was waiting for him at the farmhouse. Three police cars were parked, the way cops seem to prefer, as awkwardly as possible. One of the ambulance men wheeled Garrett's chair to the house and Pollard took over, taking him into the neat, cramped sitting room.

'Everything set?' Garrett asked.

Pollard nodded. 'I released everything after I left you. If anything's going to happen, it will be pretty soon.'

'Phone disconnected?'

'Telecom will report a fault on the line.'

'Get those RUC cars out of here. We don't want anything to frighten him off.'

Pollard looked out of the window. 'They're just pulling out,' he reported, as the police cars bumped up the track towards the road, the ambulance that had brought Garrett trundling along behind them.

'If you're worried he might do a flyover, forget it,' Pollard told him. 'Air traffic control have been alerted to inform us if anything flies in our direction.

'You've got your people in place?'

'Affirmative.'

Garrett smiled. 'Where will you be?'

'In the room above this,' Pollard said. 'Just in case.' He patted his left side near the breast pocket of his jacket to indicate that he was armed.

'No shooters, John,' Garrett said sharply. 'I want this bastard alive.'

'No matter what?'

'No matter what.'

He went out of the room and Garrett

heard him giving orders to the men he had brought with him. He looked out of the window. The cloud base was coming lower; it would rain soon. Almost as if the thought was a signal, raindrops spattered against glass. The clock on the wall sounded loud in the silence.

The setup was simple. Pollard's office had 'routinely' reported to the DCI's office in Stormont that Charles Garrett had pinpointed the location of the safe house at which Sean Hennessy and his assassination squad were hiding: Wateresk Hill Farm. Because their intelligence indicated that the IRA squad was about to move on, Garrett had whistled up a squad of shooters from the RUC Special Support Group. They would assemble at the Moneylane junction known as Five Points at midnight. Garrett was going in at four a.m.

Garrett watched the hands of the clock crawl round; three, four, five. Rain swept softly across the windows, turning the world outside into an out-of-focus snapshot. The farmer from Moneylane and his wife went stolidly about their chores; it was getting dark outside already. At about five they came inside and Garrett heard them making tea in the kitchen. Later he heard them stamp up the stairs to the safety of the bedroom.

He thought he heard a transponder crackle somewhere and spoke out loud, knowing Pollard would hear it upstairs.

'What is it?'

'ATC,' Pollard's desembodied voice reported. 'We've got a flyover.'

'Helicopter?'

'Affirmative.'

'That'll be our man,' Garrett said. 'Pass the word. Alert state red.'

'Affirmative.' He heard the faint crackle of the transceiver in the room above. He drew the curtains across the window. He imagined the big black bird somewhere in the sky above the house, the tense figure hunched over the scanner. He would know it might be a trap, but he could not take the chance it was not. He would have tried to warn Hennessy by phone, only to be told there was a fault on the line. He could not send anyone else. He had to come himself: he had no choice. If

347

Garrett captured Sean Hennessy alive, he was finished.

Garrett waited. The minute hand moved from III to VII. He heard the faint crackle of the transceiver again, then Pollard's voice, terse, tense.

'We've got a bandit.'

'Where?'

'Southwest. Coming up the hill from Maghera.'

'One man?'

'Affirmative.'

'Radio silence now. Let him run.'

'Roger.'

The finger on the clock moved from VIII to XI. Garrett sat quite still, listening, waiting. The clock bonged seven times. Its solid *tock-tack* filled the room. Then someone knocked on the door once, twice, then once-twice-thrice. After a moment, the signal was repeated. Then Garrett felt the swift touch of a cold draught as the door was opened and closed again. He heard the soft slither of a rubber-soled boot on the flagstones floor of the hallway.

'Come in, Harry,' he said.

20

It was a small funeral. There was a brief service at the church, and then the few mourners who had come to see Danny Flynn buried followed the priest and the coffin across the muddy ground to the grave.

Moira Flynn wept steadily and silently, her arms around the four children who huddled against her, puzzled expressions on their stunned faces. Man that is born of a woman is of few days, chanted the priest, and full of trouble.

After it was over they went back to the little semi, and Moira's sister Kathleen made tea. There was whiskey for the men, who sat together around the table in the dining alcove, their shoulders hunched, ignoring Garrett. The four kids went upstairs to watch telly. The oldest boy, little Danny, was twelve. He told Garrett he was going to look after his mother and his sisters now Daddy had gone away. It was always the kids who broke your heart, Garrett thought. He sat alone by the picture window looking out on the neat little front garden. Moira brought him a cup of tea and sat down on the sofa facing him.

'I just wanted to thank you, Mr Garrett,' she said. 'For arranging . . . everything.'

'There'll be a pension, Moira,' he told her. 'Not much, but something.'

'Aye,' she said, with a wry smile at her swollen belly. 'That'll make all the difference to this little fellow.'

'If I'd known what he was mixed up in . . .'

'At least you got the bastard who sold him out,' she said, and there was anger in her voice. When they heard her voice, her brother-in-law and his friends looked up. He felt their hostility coming at him like heat from a radiator. 'I only wish he was dead as well.'

'There are a lot of ways of dying,' Garrett said.

He had told her about Patterson. It was not good security, but she needed to know. He wished he could have told her how it all happened, about Harry Patterson coming into the stone-floored room in soaking camouflage kit, face smeared with black streaks, eyes as wild as a hunting panther, the big pistol cocked and levelled at Garrett's head. Then the tension went out of him like air out of a balloon. He sighed and put the gun down on the table.

'You knew,' he said. 'Hennessy told you.'

'We know it all, Patterson,' Garrett said harshly. 'Do you want to go through it with me, or would you prefer to wait for the dredgers?'

'Go to hell.'

'When did they turn you, Patterson? How long have they had you in their pocket?'

Patterson shook his head stubbornly.

'I'll tell you, then,' Garrett said. 'Almost from the start. They found out about your . . . secret life, didn't they? What happened, did someone see you coming out of the Paradise House?'

'Shut up!' Patterson shouted. 'Shut up about that!'

'All that business about women being whores was an act, wasn't it? You weren't interested in women. You never have been. You get your kicks another way, don't you, with ropes and whips and frightened young kids?'

'Shut up!' Patterson shouted again, putting his hands over his ears. 'I won't listen!'

'Once they had you, they protected you,' Garrett went on, pursuing the man relentlessly. 'That's why you hauled in Charlie Tarr and his pals, wasn't it? Your IRA friends told you one of the lads had seen you in east Belfast, but they didn't know which of them it was. When you found out it was Charlie, you arranged for him to have a little 'accident'. Am I right so far?'

Patterson looked at the gun on the table. Garrett smiled. 'Go ahead,' he said scornfully. 'It would give me a lot of pleasure to shoot you in the balls. That's if you've got balls. Maybe you're just some strange new freak the scientists haven't identified yet, some alien growth that sprouts on the inside of uncleaned toilets.'

'All right,' Patterson said. He was breathing heavily now. 'All right, that's enough.'

Garrett smiled. 'Oh, no,' he said. 'Nothing like enough.'

It took another twenty minutes of goading, insulting, sneering contempt before the dam burst and Patterson started to talk. After that it was just a matter of sitting there until it was all on tape and video, and then waiting until the security escort arrived and took him away.

It had been quite a story. When the IRA watchers reported that a senior British intelligence officer was making frequent visits to a male brothel in east Belfast, the timing was perfect for Sean Hennessy's own initiative, the punishment killing of Charles Garrett. Originally, it was to avenge Paddy McCaffery, to exact atonement for the brave lads lost in Germany, and something more: Garrett's death would be a major victory over the security services, proof that the army could reach out and kill its best high-level operatives.

Armed with information provided by Patterson, Hennessy set up the assassination of the couriers, confident that if the campaign of murder continued, PACT would take an interest and Garrett would be sent to the province. From the moment he arrived, Patterson reported Garrett's movements to Hennessy's group so that they could set up his assassination. The first attempt, on the motorway near Newtownabbey, failed because Patterson was able to obtain only incomplete details of the Elkins operation. A second attempt was mounted. Tipped off by Patterson, the murder squad would have taken the big man out at Craigantlet had it not been for the intervention of Patricia Burke. As for Garrett's plan to take him at Craigthomas, Hennessy had known about it from the moment it was set in motion at security headquarters. Only May Nolan's astonishment at recognizing Patterson had saved Garrett's life. When Patterson put a bullet in her head he looked like a hero; in fact, he was making sure his own skin was safe. The same was true in the case of Danny Flynn. Patterson had sold the little man's life as callously as another might step on a bug.

'I'll have to be going, Moira,' Garrett said, getting up.

'You'll be going back to England,' she said. 'Home?'

He nodded. 'My work here is done.'

'Do they care over there, Charles? Does anyone care about us?'

He did not answer her. He wasn't even sure he could. She nodded, as if his silence was answer enough.

'I sometimes think our grief causes as little heartbreak in England as do the tears of British women when viewed from here,' she said. 'Goodbye, Charles. Thank you for coming. Danny would be glad to know you were here.'

'You'll keep in touch with me, won't you? Let me know how the kids are?'

'Of course I will,' she said warmly, but he knew he would never see or hear from her again. He was not a member of her clan, of any clan in this sad, grey, war-weary city. He put on his trenchcoat and the battered Donegal tweed hat. It was pouring with rain outside.

He drove back up to the security complex at Stormont and turned in the car. Stephen Elkins was waiting for him when he got upstairs.

'Came over specially to say goodbye, old chap,' he said expansively. 'Just wanted to say, well done.'

Garrett smiled. 'Well, thanks, Elkins.'

'How's the old side? Healed up?'

'More or less,' Garrett said. 'The doctor was right. I can tell when it's going to rain.'

'I take it you heard about Patterson?'

Garrett felt a chill of precognition. 'What about him?'

'Hanged himself in his cell,' Elkins said. 'During interrogation.'

The words said one thing; the evasive eyes said something totally different. Garrett remembered the cynical saw: military justice is to justice as military music is to music. Poor bastard, he thought. Spying for the IRA wasn't like spying for the Russians. If you were blown, nobody put you on a plane for Moscow, where a medal and a pension and a little flat would be waiting for you. There was nowhere to run in Ireland. Patterson's death had been inevitable from the second Patricia Burke's bullet put an end to the life of Sean Hennessy. What was ironic was that Patterson died not even knowing it had happened.

Garrett walked across to the window and watched the rain drumming on the panes. 'Is there anything else we have to cover before I leave?' he said over his shoulder.

'I don't think so,' Elkins said. 'What plane are you catching?'

Garrett checked the schedule. 'There's one at four-thirty,' he said. 'If I get a move on, I can just make it.'

Elkins held out his hand. 'Good trip,' he said. There was no warmth in his voice. It was clear that he felt he had won something, whatever it was. And as equally clear he would not forget being excluded from Garrett's confidence. Garrett nodded and went down to the car. The driver put on the radio for the four o'clock news. The announcer reported that Patrick McAuliffe, aged thirty-nine, a garage mechanic, had been shot dead while talking to a friend outside a pub in the Springfield Road. A second man had been wounded in the leg. Police believed Loyalist gunmen were responsible for the attack.

Another casualty, he thought, in a war so dirty it didn't even have a name.

★   ★   ★

Returning to London from Belfast was like arriving in Paris after a week in Lille. The British Airways 757 left behind the blustery winds and slanting rain that had been punishing Northern Ireland for ten days and deposited its passengers at a Heathrow glowing in the sunset of a lovely autumn day. Garrett came out of the customs hall to see Jessica waiting by the barrier with a cardboard sign on which, in big felt-tipped letters, was printed the legend 'YOUR PLACE OR MINE?' He smiled, feeling the depression that had sat on his shoulders all the way across the Irish Sea lifting.

'Yours,' he said, and hugged her close. She smelled gorgeous: Nina Ricci's *L' Air du Temps*, he thought.

'Thought you'd say that,' she said. 'Your wish is my command.'

She was wearing her tan Four Seasons raincoat and what he called her *Snows of Kilimanjaro* hat. She drove into town fast but well, moving decisively through the town traffic. She parked in the underground park beneath Cadogan Place, and they crossed the street to her flat. She closed the door behind them and he took her in his arms and kissed her.

'Thanks,' she said. 'I needed that.'

'We give a reduction for quantity,' he said.

She grinned like an urchin and shook her head. 'First, get out of that damned uniform. I'll run a hot bath for you. While you're soaking Northern Ireland out of your system, I'll open this 'ere bottle of Krug wot I just 'appen to have chilled in case of gentleman callers.'

He went into the bedroom and stripped to the skin, putting on the silk dressing gown hanging behind the door. He padded through to the bathroom. It was warm and steamy and smelled of herbs.

'I put in some Badedas,' Jessica grinned. 'It says on the bottle it gives you lebenslust. I hope.'

He slid into the hot bath with a groan of pleasure. The new scars on his side throbbed to remind him that although the wounds were healed, it would be a while longer before he could disregard them. Jessica came back in carrying two flutes of champagne. She handed one to him and they clinked glasses.

'I'd scrub your back,' she said, 'but some food out there needs me more.'

'I'll manage,' he told her. 'Go and cook.'

He lay soaking until she called his name. Then he got out and towelled himself dry, putting on the underwear, shirt and trousers she had laid out on the chair. He put on a pair of socks and slipped on the Bruno Magli casuals, then spent another five minutes having a particularly close shave before joining her for a second glass of champagne in the kitchen.

'Smells good,' he said, lifting a pan lid. 'What is it?'

'Wait and see,' she told him, slapping his hand. 'Go and pour the wine.'

The circular dining table was laid for two, with a small floral arrangement in the middle and single blue candles in silver holders at each side of it. Matching blue napkins were folded on the side plates. A bottle of '83 Pommerol lay in a basket, a corkscrew alongside it. He opened the wine and put it to one side; 'letting it breathe' was a nonsense he had no time for, but he wanted to wait for Jessica. She came through from the kitchen carrying a tray, and from it put some silver dishes on the table.

'Fresh spinach,' she announced. '*Pommes duchesse*. And — ta-daaah!'

She lifted the lid of the largest of the dishes, and a strong aroma rose from it. 'Pheasant?' he said.

'Braised in cranberries and fresh ginger, with orange juice, mushrooms and red wine.'

'If it tastes as good as it sounds, it will be delicious,' he said. 'And speaking of red wine . . . ' He poured some of the Pommerol into the glasses. It was rich and dark red and tasted of oak and blackcurrant. They raised their glasses. 'My compliments to the chef,' he said.

'Wait till you see what's for dessert,' she told him.

Much, much later, after they had made love, she saw the fresh scars, the two-inch weal under his arm, the puckered circle just above his left hip.

'Souvenirs,' he said. 'From Ireland.'

'Oh, Charles,' she said, and all at once she was crying. 'Why do you do it? Why does it have to be you all the time?'

He held her in his arms. 'We've talked about this before, Jess,' he said softly. 'You know why.'

She sat up and put on the light. Her body looked like carved ivory in the soft light. 'Let's go and finish that champagne,' she said. He got up, put on his robe and padded across the hall after her. She got the wine out of the refrigerator and took two glasses out of a cupboard. She poured each of them a glassful and then leaned back against the work top.

'What is it, Charles? What was different this time?' she asked.

'Did I say something was different?'

'You didn't have to. Tell me.'

He told her. He told her about all of it, Elkins and Patterson, Danny Flynn and Patricia Burke. And, finally, about Sean Hennessy. When he finished talking, he felt empty, bereft, as if all his emotions had been siphoned off. He sighed and put down the wine glass.

'And now it's over, Jess. All of it, over.'

The words alone meant nothing. But she knew what he was really trying to tell her: that at long last, he had laid the memory of Diana Garrett's death to rest. But she knew there was something more: in spite of what he said, it wasn't over. Not yet.

'I'm a fool,' she whispered, putting her arms around him. 'I should have known. It's Hennessy, isn't it? He's been here with us the whole time, ever since you came back. Like a ghost.'

'How did you know?'

'Because I love you. Don't hold out on me, Charles.'

'I'm sorry.'

She smiled. Her eyes were like starry pools he could drown in. She kissed him softly.

'Just remember we're us. Us, Charles. Not you over there and me over here.'

'And the ghosts?' he said.

'Trust me,' Jessica said. 'I know how to handle ghosts.'

'You do?'

The smile turned to a hoyden grin, and a devil he had seen before danced in the darkness of her eyes.

'Oh, yes,' she whispered as she switched off the light. 'Come back to bed and I'll show you.'

THE END

We do hope that you have enjoyed reading this large print book.

Did you know that all of our titles are available for purchase?

We publish a wide range of high quality large print books including:
Romances, Mysteries, Classics
General Fiction
Non Fiction and Westerns

Special interest titles available in large print are:
The Little Oxford Dictionary
Music Book, Song Book
Hymn Book, Service Book

Also available from us courtesy of Oxford University Press:
Young Readers' Dictionary
(large print edition)
Young Readers' Thesaurus
(large print edition)

For further information or a free brochure, please contact us at:
Ulverscroft Large Print Books Ltd.,
The Green, Bradgate Road, Anstey,
Leicester, LE7 7FU, England.
Tel: (00 44) **0116 236 4325**
Fax: (00 44) **0116 234 0205**

Other titles in the
Linford Mystery Library:

THE FROZEN LIMIT

John Russell Fearn

Defying the edict of the Medical Council, Dr. Robert Cranston, helped by Dr. Campbell, carries out an unauthorised medical experiment with a 'deep freeze' system of suspended animation. The volunteer is Claire Baxter, an attractive film stunt-girl. But when Claire undergoes deep freeze unconsciousness, the two doctors discover that they cannot restore the girl. She is barely alive. Despite every endeavour to revive the girl, nothing happens, and Cranston and Campbell find themselves charged with murder . . .

THE SECRET POLICEMAN

Rafe McGregor

When a superintendent in the Security Branch is murdered, top detective Jack Forrester is assigned to the case. Realising his new colleagues are keeping vital information from him, Jack Forrester sets out to catch the killer on his own. But Forrester soon becomes ensnared in a web of drug traffickers, Moslem vigilantes, and international terrorists. As he delves deeper into the superintendent's past, he realises he must make an arrest quickly — before he becomes the next police casualty . . .

THE SPACE-BORN

E. C. Tubb

Jay West was a killer — he had to be. No human kindness could swerve him from duty, because the ironclad law of the Space Ship was that no one — *no one* — ever must live past forty! But how could he fulfil his next assignment — the murder of his sweetheart's father? Yet, how could he *not* do it? The old had to make way for the new generations. There was no air, no food, and no room for the old . . .